The Crime Syndicate

Thrillers, Volume 3

William James Brown

Published by Serene Sky Publishing, 2024.

THE CRIME SYNDICATE

First edition. November 24, 2024.

Copyright © 2024 William James Brown.

ISBN: 979-8230498711

Written by William James Brown.

Table of Contents

To those who fight against the shadows,

To the relentless guardians of justice,

And to the unsung heroes who risk everything for the truth.

This book is dedicated to the brave men and women

Who stand firm against the tide of corruption,

And to those who have paid the ultimate price

In the pursuit of a safer, better world.

May your courage inspire others,

And may your sacrifices never be forgotten.

Chapter 1: The Underworld Awakens

Detective Jack Thompson stood on the rooftop of his apartment building, his sharp blue eyes scanning the city below. The sprawling metropolis of Bay City lay sprawled out before him, a labyrinth of neon lights and darkened alleyways. From this vantage point, he could almost forget the rot that festered in the heart of the city, but the illusion was always fleeting. The real Bay City was down there, in the streets, where shadows moved with sinister purpose and danger lurked around every corner.

Jack was a man in his early forties, with a square jaw that hadn't seen a razor in days, and short, dark hair that was just beginning to gray at the temples. His build was solid, a testament to years spent in the police force, and his demeanor was one of quiet intensity. He had been a detective for almost two decades, and in that time, he had seen Bay City change. Crime had always been a problem, but in recent years, it had escalated to unprecedented levels. The police were fighting a losing battle against an enemy that was always one step ahead.

Bay City had always been a melting pot of cultures and ambitions. It was a place where dreams were chased and often shattered. The wealth disparity was stark; gleaming skyscrapers of the business district contrasted sharply with the dilapidated tenements of the poorer neighborhoods. It was in these forgotten corners of the city that the crime syndicates flourished, exploiting the desperate and disenfranchised.

Jack's phone buzzed in his pocket, breaking his reverie. He glanced at the screen and saw a message from his partner, Detective Lisa Ramirez. She was waiting for him at the precinct. With a resigned sigh, he pocketed the phone and made his way down the fire escape to the street below.

As he navigated the crowded sidewalks, Jack couldn't help but notice the tension in the air. People moved quickly, heads down, avoiding eye contact. The city's residents were on edge, and for good reason. The recent surge in violent crime had left everyone feeling vulnerable. Jack reached the precinct, a nondescript building that looked like any other on the block. Inside, it was a hive of activity. Officers moved with purpose, phones rang incessantly, and the hum of conversation filled the air.

Lisa was waiting for him in their shared office, a small room cluttered with case files and whiteboards covered in scribbled notes. She looked up as he entered, her dark eyes serious.

"Jack, we've got a new case," she said without preamble. "Another body was found in the Southside docks."

Jack nodded, his expression grim. The Southside docks had become a dumping ground for the city's unwanted. It was the third body found there in as many weeks.

"Any leads?" he asked, pulling up a chair.

"Not much," Lisa admitted. "Same as the others. No ID, no witnesses. But this one's different. There was a message left at the scene."

Jack raised an eyebrow. "A message?"

Lisa handed him a photograph. It showed a piece of paper pinned to the victim's chest with a knife. The message was simple: "The Wolf is watching."

Jack felt a chill run down his spine. The Wolf. The name had been whispered in the criminal underworld for months, but no one knew who he was or what he wanted. He was an enigma, a ghost. His influence was felt everywhere, yet he remained invisible.

"We need to find out who this Wolf is," Jack said, his voice determined. "And fast."

Lisa nodded in agreement. "I've already put out feelers. We'll see if anyone's willing to talk."

As they prepared to head to the crime scene, Jack couldn't shake the feeling that they were up against something far bigger than they realized. The Wolf was no ordinary criminal. He was organized, methodical, and ruthless. And he had the city in a stranglehold.

The drive to the Southside docks was a somber one. The area was a maze of warehouses and shipping containers, a place where the city's poor and forgotten eked out a living. The docks were a stark contrast to the gleaming towers of the financial district, a reminder of the city's deep-seated inequality.

The crime scene was cordoned off, and uniformed officers were keeping curious onlookers at bay. Jack and Lisa flashed their badges and ducked under the tape. The victim lay sprawled on the ground, a young man in his twenties. His face was a mask of terror, eyes wide open in death.

Jack crouched down beside the body, examining the message pinned to the man's chest. "The Wolf is watching." It was a taunt, a challenge.

"Whoever this Wolf is, he's trying to send a message," Jack said, standing up. "He wants us to know he's in control."

Lisa nodded, her expression thoughtful. "But why leave a message this time? The previous victims didn't have any."

"Maybe he's getting bolder," Jack suggested. "Or maybe he wants to draw us out, make us chase him."

As they worked the scene, Jack couldn't shake the feeling that they were being watched. The hairs on the back of his neck stood up, and he scanned the area, but saw nothing out of the ordinary. Still, the feeling persisted.

By the time they finished, the sun was setting, casting long shadows over the docks. Jack and Lisa returned to the precinct, their minds racing with questions. Who was the Wolf? What was his endgame? And how could they stop him before he struck again?

The next few days were a blur of interviews, stakeouts, and dead ends. The city's criminal underworld was tight-lipped, and fear of the Wolf kept potential informants silent. Every lead seemed to end in a brick wall.

Jack found himself spending more and more time at the precinct, pouring over case files and trying to piece together the puzzle. He knew they were missing something, some crucial piece of information that would unlock the whole case.

Late one night, as he was going through yet another stack of files, his phone buzzed. It was a message from an unknown number. "Meet me at the old warehouse on 5th. Midnight. Come alone."

Jack's instincts screamed trap, but he knew he had to take the chance. He grabbed his coat and headed out, leaving a note for Lisa in case things went south.

The warehouse on 5th was a relic from a bygone era, its crumbling facade a testament to the city's industrial past. Jack approached cautiously, his hand resting on the butt of his gun. The air was thick with tension as he stepped inside.

A single light illuminated the vast, empty space. In the center of the room stood a figure, shrouded in shadow. Jack couldn't make out any details, but he could feel the man's eyes on him.

"You're the detective looking for the Wolf," the man said, his voice low and gravelly.

"I am," Jack replied, trying to keep his voice steady. "Who are you?"

"Call me a concerned citizen," the man said. "I have information you need."

Jack stepped closer, his eyes narrowing. "Why should I trust you?"

The man chuckled, a sound devoid of humor. "You don't have to. But if you want to catch the Wolf, you'll listen."

Jack listened as the man laid out the details of the Wolf's operations. The syndicate was vast, with its tentacles reaching into every corner of the city. Drugs, extortion, human trafficking – the Wolf had his hands in it all. And he was untouchable because he always stayed in the shadows, using intermediaries to do his dirty work.

"The Wolf is planning something big," the man said. "I don't know what, but it's going to shake this city to its core."

"How do I find him?" Jack asked, his heart pounding.

The man handed him a slip of paper. "This is the address of one of his safe houses. Start there."

Before Jack could ask any more questions, the man slipped away into the darkness, leaving him alone in the empty warehouse. Jack pocketed the paper and hurried back to the precinct. He had a lead, and time was running out.

The next morning, Jack and Lisa, armed with a warrant, raided the address provided by the informant. The safe house was a modest apartment in a run-down building on the city's outskirts. Inside, they found a treasure trove of information – documents, photos, and computer files detailing the syndicate's operations.

As they combed through the evidence, a clearer picture of the Wolf began to emerge. He was meticulous, careful to cover his tracks, but there were gaps, small clues that pointed to his true identity.

Jack's excitement grew as they pieced together the puzzle. They were getting closer, but the Wolf was still one step ahead. They needed a break, something that would give them an edge.

Their break came in the form of a frantic phone call from one of their informants. The Wolf was planning a major drug shipment, and they had a location and time. It was their chance to catch him in the act.

The night of the bust, Jack and Lisa assembled a team and moved in on the warehouse where the shipment was scheduled to take place. They moved quietly, their senses on high alert.

The warehouse was dark, but they could hear voices and the sounds of movement inside. Jack signaled for his team to move in, and they burst through the doors, weapons drawn.

The scene that greeted them was chaotic. Men scattered in all directions, and shots rang out as the police moved to secure the area. Jack's heart pounded as he scanned the faces, looking for the Wolf.

In the midst of the chaos, a figure moved with purpose, directing the others. Jack's breath caught in his throat as he recognized the man from the description in the files. It was the Wolf.

Jack moved through the fray, his eyes locked on his target. The Wolf saw him and hesitated for a moment before turning and running. Jack gave chase, his determination fueled by the knowledge that this was their chance to bring down the syndicate.

The chase led them through the maze of shipping containers and out into the open. The Wolf was fast, but Jack was faster. He tackled the man to the ground, and they struggled for control.

The Wolf was a formidable opponent, but Jack's years of training gave him the edge. He managed to pin the man down and cuff him, his breath coming in ragged gasps.

"It's over," Jack said, his voice filled with triumph. "You're done."

The Wolf looked up at him, his eyes filled with a mix of fury and resignation. "You have no idea what you've done," he said. "This is far from over."

As the other officers moved in to secure the scene, Jack couldn't shake the feeling that the Wolf's words were a dire warning. They had won a battle, but the war was far from over.

The arrest of the Wolf sent shockwaves through Bay City. The media hailed it as a major victory in the fight against organized crime, but Jack knew better. The Wolf had been a formidable opponent, but he was just one piece of a much larger puzzle.

In the days that followed, the police worked tirelessly to dismantle the syndicate's operations. They raided safe houses, arrested key members, and seized assets. It was a massive effort, but Jack couldn't shake the feeling that they were still missing something.

His suspicions were confirmed when he received a call from Sarah, the undercover agent. She had managed to escape the syndicate's clutches and had crucial information about their next move.

Jack and Lisa met Sarah at a safe house, where she detailed the syndicate's plans. The Wolf had been part of a larger organization, a network of crime syndicates working together to control the city. And they had a contingency plan in place, one that could bring the city to its knees.

"We need to act fast," Sarah said, her voice urgent. "They're planning something big, and if we don't stop them, it could be catastrophic."

Jack's mind raced as he processed the information. The Wolf had been a major player, but the real threat was still out there. They needed to find the leaders of this network and take them down before it was too late.

The next few weeks were a blur of activity as Jack, Lisa, and Sarah worked to uncover the identities of the syndicate's leaders. It was a dangerous game, and they knew that one wrong move could cost them everything.

Their efforts paid off when they identified the leaders and their base of operations. It was a heavily fortified compound on the outskirts of the city, and taking it down would require a coordinated assault.

The night of the raid, Jack and his team moved in with military precision. The compound was heavily guarded, but they were ready. They moved through the perimeter, neutralizing guards and breaching the defenses.

Inside, they found the leaders gathered in a conference room, discussing their plans. The element of surprise was on their side, and they moved quickly to apprehend the men.

As the leaders were taken into custody, Jack felt a sense of relief. They had struck a major blow against the syndicate, but he knew that the fight was far from over. The network was vast, and there were still many who would try to fill the power vacuum.

As they left the compound, Jack couldn't help but feel a sense of hope. They had made significant progress, but the real battle was just beginning. Bay City was still plagued by crime, and the fight to reclaim it would be long and arduous.

But Jack was ready. He had faced the darkness and come out the other side. He knew the road ahead would be tough, but he was determined to see it through. For the sake of the city he loved, and for the people who called it home.

As the sun rose over Bay City, Jack stood on the rooftop of the precinct, looking out over the city. The battle against the underworld was far from over, but he was ready for whatever came next. The city had awakened, and so had he. Together, they would face the challenges ahead and emerge stronger.

The fight against the crime syndicate was just beginning, but Jack knew that as long as he had his team by his side, they could overcome anything. The city was worth fighting for, and he would do whatever it took to protect it.

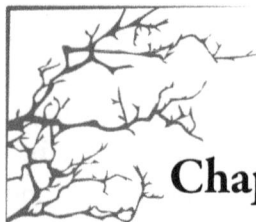

Chapter 2: A Bloody Message

Bay City was no stranger to crime, but this was different. This was brazen. In the heart of downtown, amidst the glittering towers and bustling streets, a high-profile assassination had just rocked the city's very core. The victim: billionaire philanthropist Richard Helms, a man known for his charitable contributions and his efforts to revitalize the very city that now lay in shock.

Detective Jack Thompson sat in his car, staring at the towering skyline as the morning sun cast long shadows. His phone buzzed incessantly with updates and notifications, but he ignored them for the moment, lost in thought. The murder of Richard Helms wasn't just another case; it was a statement. And the city would be watching their every move.

Jack's partner, Detective Lisa Ramirez, approached the car, her face set in a grim expression. "Jack, we need to get moving. The scene's already swarming with media."

Jack nodded, snapping out of his reverie. "Let's go."

They navigated through the congested streets, sirens blaring, pushing through the throngs of curious onlookers and reporters. When they arrived at the scene, the air was thick with tension. Police tape cordoned off a luxurious penthouse, now a crime scene, and officers were busy trying to maintain order.

As they stepped out of the car, they were greeted by Captain Reed, a grizzled veteran who had seen more than his fair share of violence. "Thompson, Ramirez, glad you're here. This one's bad. Real bad."

Jack and Lisa followed Reed into the building, past the opulent lobby and up to the top floor. The penthouse was a testament to wealth and power, with floor-to-ceiling windows offering a panoramic view of the city. But all that splendor was marred by the grim scene before them.

Richard Helms lay sprawled on the floor, his lifeless eyes staring at the ceiling. The white marble was stained with his blood, and a sense of unease permeated the room. For a moment, Jack felt a pang of sadness. Helms had been one of the few genuinely good men in a city riddled with corruption. His loss was a blow not just to those who knew him, but to Bay City itself.

Lisa moved to examine the body, her trained eyes taking in every detail. "Single gunshot wound to the chest. Close range. Whoever did this wanted to send a message."

"Speaking of which," Reed said, handing Jack a piece of paper. "This was found on his desk."

Jack unfolded the paper, revealing a cryptic message written in neat, precise handwriting:

"The Wolf sends his regards."

Jack's heart sank. The Wolf again. This wasn't just an assassination; it was a declaration of war.

"Looks like our old friend is back," Lisa muttered, reading over Jack's shoulder.

Jack nodded. "And he's getting bolder. We need to figure out what he wants, and fast."

The scene was meticulously processed, with forensic teams collecting evidence and photographing every inch of the penthouse. Jack and Lisa interviewed the building's staff, but no one had seen or heard anything unusual. It was as if the killer had slipped in and out without a trace.

Back at the precinct, the atmosphere was charged with urgency. The news of Helms' assassination had spread like wildfire, and the pressure to solve the case was immense. Jack and Lisa retreated to their office, sifting through the information they had gathered.

"Let's start with the coded message," Jack said, pinning it to the whiteboard. "What do we know about the Wolf's MO?"

Lisa tapped her pen thoughtfully. "He's meticulous, methodical. Always leaves a calling card, but this is the first time he's left a message like this."

"Why Helms?" Jack wondered aloud. "What did he have that the Wolf wanted?"

"Power, influence," Lisa suggested. "Helms was more than just a philanthropist. He had connections in high places, both legal and otherwise."

Jack frowned. "Then there's more to this than just a murder. It's about control. The Wolf wants to send a message to the city's elite."

Their discussion was interrupted by a knock on the door. Sarah Miller, the undercover agent who had infiltrated the syndicate, walked in. She looked tired but determined.

"I heard about Helms," she said, taking a seat. "This isn't just about making a statement. The Wolf has a plan, and Helms was in his way."

"Do you know what that plan is?" Jack asked.

Sarah shook her head. "Not yet. But I know someone who might. There's a man named Marcus Voss. He's a middleman for the syndicate, handles their finances. If anyone knows what the Wolf is planning, it's him."

"Where can we find him?" Lisa asked.

"Last I heard, he was laying low in one of the syndicate's safe houses in the East End," Sarah replied. "But be careful. Voss is paranoid, and he won't go down without a fight."

Jack and Lisa exchanged a glance. This was the break they needed.

"Let's go," Jack said, grabbing his coat. "It's time to pay Mr. Voss a visit."

The East End of Bay City was a stark contrast to the glitz and glamour of downtown. It was a place where the city's poorest struggled to survive, and crime was a way of life. The streets were narrow and winding, lined with dilapidated buildings and makeshift markets.

They arrived at the safe house, a nondescript building that blended in with its surroundings. Jack and Lisa moved cautiously, their guns drawn. The door was slightly ajar, and they slipped inside, their senses on high alert.

The interior was dark and cluttered, filled with the detritus of a man on the run. Papers were scattered everywhere, and the air was thick with the smell of stale cigarettes. They moved through the rooms, their footsteps echoing in the silence.

In the back room, they found Marcus Voss. He was sitting at a table, a gun in his hand, his eyes wide with fear. He looked like a cornered animal, ready to fight to the death.

"Put the gun down, Voss," Jack said calmly. "We just want to talk."

Voss shook his head, his hand trembling. "You don't understand. The Wolf... he'll kill me if I talk."

"He'll kill you if you don't," Lisa countered. "We can protect you, but you need to tell us what you know."

For a moment, it seemed like Voss might comply. But then he lunged at them, his gun raised. Jack fired a single shot, hitting Voss in the shoulder. The man cried out in pain, dropping his weapon.

They quickly secured him, and Jack knelt beside him. "Voss, listen to me. You have a chance to get out of this alive, but you need to help us."

Voss groaned, his face contorted in pain. "Alright, alright. I'll talk."

They transported Voss back to the precinct and patched him up. In the interrogation room, he sat slumped in a chair, his face pale.

"The Wolf... he's planning something big," Voss said, his voice weak. "Helms was just the beginning. He's targeting the city's power structure, taking out anyone who stands in his way."

"What does he want?" Jack asked.

"Control," Voss replied. "He wants to control the city's underworld, and he's willing to do whatever it takes to get it. He's already got the gangs in his pocket, and now he's going after the politicians and businessmen."

"How do we stop him?" Lisa asked.

Voss shook his head. "I don't know. The Wolf... he's smart. He's always one step ahead. But there's one thing. He's planning a major hit, something that'll cripple the city."

"Where and when?" Jack demanded.

Voss hesitated, his eyes filled with fear. "The city council meeting. Tomorrow night. He's going to hit it hard, make an example of them."

Jack and Lisa exchanged a grim look. They had less than twenty-four hours to prevent a catastrophe.

They worked through the night, coordinating with other law enforcement agencies to secure the city council building. The atmosphere was tense, and the weight of the responsibility hung heavy on their shoulders. Failure was not an option.

The next evening, the city council building was a fortress. Officers were stationed at every entrance, and the surrounding streets were cordoned off. Jack and Lisa were inside, monitoring the situation closely.

As the meeting began, Jack couldn't shake the feeling that something was off. The Wolf was cunning, and he wouldn't launch an attack unless he was sure of success. They had to be missing something.

Suddenly, there was a commotion outside. A delivery truck had pulled up to the building, and the driver was arguing with the officers. Jack's instincts screamed danger.

"Check that truck," he ordered.

The officers moved in, but it was too late. The truck exploded, sending a shockwave through the area. The building shook, and the power went out, plunging them into darkness.

Chaos erupted as people scrambled for safety. Jack and Lisa fought their way through the panic, their minds racing. This had been a diversion, a way to draw their attention away from the real target.

They made their way to the council chamber, where the members were huddled in fear. The room was filled with smoke, and the air was thick with tension.

"Everyone, stay calm," Jack shouted. "We're getting you out of here."

As they moved to evacuate the council members, gunfire erupted from the shadows. The Wolf's men had infiltrated the building, and a firefight ensued. Jack and Lisa returned fire, their hearts pounding with adrenaline.

In the chaos, Jack spotted a figure moving with purpose. The Wolf. He was headed for the council president, a man who had been outspoken against organized crime.

"Lisa, cover me," Jack yelled, breaking into a run.

He tackled the Wolf just as he raised his gun, and they grappled on the floor. The Wolf was strong, but Jack fought with the desperation of a man who had everything to lose.

With a final burst of strength, Jack managed to pin the Wolf down, cuffing him. "It's over," he said, his voice filled with determination.

The Wolf laughed, a chilling sound. "You think this changes anything? There are others, more like me. This city will never be free."

"Maybe not," Jack replied. "But as long as there are people willing to fight, there's hope."

The Wolf was taken into custody, and the city council members were safely evacuated. The immediate threat had been neutralized, but Jack knew the battle was far from over.

As dawn broke over Bay City, Jack and Lisa stood outside the building, exhausted but resolute. They had won a victory, but the war against the underworld would continue.

"We did it," Lisa said, her voice filled with relief.

"Yeah," Jack replied, his eyes on the horizon. "But this is just the beginning."

The assassination of Richard Helms had sent shockwaves through the city, but it had also galvanized those who were willing to stand up against the darkness. Jack knew that the fight would be long and hard, but he was ready. For the city, for its people, and for the hope of a better future.

As they walked away from the council building, Jack felt a sense of determination. The Wolf had been a formidable opponent, but there would be others. And as long as he had Lisa by his side, he knew they could face whatever came next.

The city was waking up, and with it, a renewed sense of purpose. The fight for Bay City had only just begun, and Jack was ready to lead the charge.

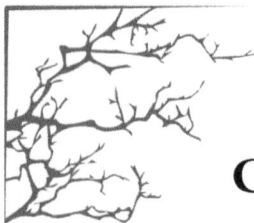

Chapter 3: Deep Cover

Undercover agent Sarah Miller had been living in the shadows for nearly a year. As she stepped out of the dilapidated apartment she had come to call home, the weight of her dual life pressed heavily on her shoulders. In the criminal underworld, she was known as Rebecca Turner, a street-smart hustler with a knack for staying one step ahead of the law. In reality, she was a highly skilled FBI agent, tasked with infiltrating one of the most dangerous crime syndicates Bay City had ever seen.

Sarah had joined the syndicate by posing as a down-on-her-luck woman looking for protection and a place to belong. Her entry into their ranks had been facilitated by a carefully crafted backstory and a series of staged encounters that had earned her the trust of some low-level members. From there, she had gradually worked her way up, gaining the confidence of those in power. Now, she was deep within the inner circle, surrounded by danger at every turn.

Her mornings began like any other. She carefully maintained the facade of her alter ego, meticulously checking for any signs of surveillance or suspicion from her criminal counterparts. Every interaction, every conversation was a potential threat to her cover. One wrong move, one slip of the tongue, and her life could be forfeit. But the stakes were too high to back out now. She was the key to bringing down the syndicate from the inside, and she knew it.

As she walked through the narrow, trash-strewn streets of the East End, she was acutely aware of the eyes that followed her. The neighborhood was a stronghold of the syndicate, a place where the law held little sway. It was a world unto itself, governed by the rules of the underworld. Trust was a rare commodity, and betrayal was met with swift and brutal retribution.

Sarah's destination was a run-down warehouse that served as the syndicate's headquarters. From the outside, it appeared abandoned, but inside, it was a hive of activity. Men and women moved with purpose, their expressions hard and their eyes wary. This was the nerve center of the organization, where deals were made, orders were given, and lives were ended.

As she entered the warehouse, she was greeted by Dominic Russo, one of the syndicate's top lieutenants. Dominic was a hulking figure, his muscular frame and tattooed arms giving him an intimidating presence. He was fiercely loyal to the syndicate, and his ruthless efficiency had earned him a reputation as someone not to be crossed.

"Morning, Rebecca," Dominic said, his voice a low rumble. "Boss wants to see you."

Sarah nodded, masking the flicker of apprehension that ran through her. "Thanks, Dom. I'll head up now."

She made her way to the office on the second floor, her mind racing. The "boss" was Viktor Ivanov, the enigmatic leader of the syndicate, known to his enemies as "The Wolf." Viktor was a man of few words, but his actions spoke volumes. He ruled with an iron fist, and his intelligence and cunning had made him a formidable adversary.

As Sarah entered Viktor's office, she was struck by the contrast between the opulence of the room and the squalor outside. The walls were lined with expensive art, and the furniture was sleek and modern. Viktor sat behind a large mahogany desk, his piercing blue eyes studying her intently.

"Rebecca," he said, his voice smooth and controlled. "I have a task for you."

Sarah's heart pounded in her chest. "What do you need, boss?"

"We have a problem," Viktor said, leaning back in his chair. "The police are getting too close. We have a rat in our midst, and I need you to find out who it is."

Sarah felt a surge of panic, but she forced herself to remain calm. "Any leads?"

Viktor shook his head. "No. But I trust you to handle this discreetly. We can't afford any more mistakes."

"I'll take care of it," Sarah promised, hoping her voice didn't betray her anxiety.

Viktor nodded, satisfied. "Good. Report back to me as soon as you have something."

As she left the office, Sarah's mind raced. The pressure to maintain her cover had just increased tenfold. She needed to find a way to divert suspicion from herself while continuing to gather intelligence for Jack and Lisa. The delicate balance of her dual life was becoming increasingly precarious.

Back at her apartment, Sarah took a deep breath and allowed herself a moment of vulnerability. She reached for her phone, a lifeline to the outside world, and sent a coded message to her handler at the FBI. It was a simple update, but it conveyed the urgency of her situation. She knew she would need to meet with Jack and Lisa soon, but arranging a covert meeting without arousing suspicion would be a challenge.

The following days were a blur of activity as Sarah worked to identify potential suspects within the syndicate. She interviewed members, reviewed records, and subtly planted seeds of doubt to shift the focus away from herself. It was a dangerous game, and the tension was palpable. Every interaction felt like walking a tightrope over a pit of vipers.

One evening, as Sarah was combing through files in the warehouse, she overheard a conversation that sent chills down her spine. Dominic and another lieutenant, Carlos, were discussing plans for a major operation. The details were vague, but it was clear that something big was in the works. Sarah knew she had to get this information to Jack and Lisa, but the risk was enormous.

She waited until late at night, when the warehouse was quiet and most of the members had left. Moving silently, she made her way to a hidden storage room she had discovered weeks earlier. It was a small, cramped space, but it provided a modicum of privacy. She pulled out her phone and composed a message to Jack.

"Urgent. Major operation planned. Need to meet ASAP."

She hit send and hoped that Jack would understand the gravity of the situation. As she slipped the phone back into her pocket, she heard footsteps approaching. Her heart leapt into her throat, and she quickly moved to a stack of crates, trying to blend into the shadows.

Dominic entered the room, his expression wary. He glanced around, but didn't see her. After a moment, he left, and Sarah exhaled in relief. She had narrowly avoided discovery, but the close call only heightened her sense of urgency.

The next day, Sarah received a message from Jack. They had arranged a meeting at a secluded location on the outskirts of the city. It was a risky move, but she knew it was necessary. She made her way to the meeting point, a deserted warehouse near the docks, and waited.

Jack and Lisa arrived shortly after, their expressions tense but relieved to see her. They quickly embraced, the weight of their shared burden evident in their eyes.

"Sarah, are you okay?" Jack asked, his concern palpable.

"I'm fine," Sarah replied, though she felt anything but. "We don't have much time. The syndicate is planning something big. I overheard Dominic and Carlos talking about a major operation, but I don't have all the details yet."

Lisa frowned. "Do you think it's connected to Helms' assassination?"

Sarah nodded. "It has to be. The timing is too coincidental. Viktor is tightening his grip, and he's paranoid about leaks. He's tasked me with finding the rat, so I have to be extra careful."

Jack ran a hand through his hair, frustration evident. "We need more information. Without knowing what they're planning, we're flying blind."

"I know," Sarah said, her voice strained. "I'm doing everything I can, but it's getting harder to stay under the radar. If Viktor finds out I'm the mole, I'm as good as dead."

"We'll protect you," Jack said firmly. "But we need to act fast. Can you get us anything concrete?"

Sarah hesitated, then nodded. "I'll try. There's a shipment coming in tonight. It might be related to the operation. I can get the details and let you know."

"Be careful," Lisa said, her eyes filled with worry. "We can't afford to lose you."

Sarah smiled weakly. "I'll do my best."

As they parted ways, Sarah felt a renewed sense of determination. The stakes were higher than ever, but she was resolved to see this through. She returned to the syndicate's headquarters, her mind focused on the task at hand.

That night, Sarah shadowed Dominic and Carlos as they prepared for the shipment. She stayed hidden, watching as they coordinated with their contacts and arranged for the delivery. It was a tense, nerve-wracking process, but she managed to gather crucial information.

As the shipment arrived, Sarah saw that it consisted of high-grade weapons and explosives. The realization hit her like a punch to the gut. This wasn't just a routine operation; it was a full-scale assault. The syndicate was gearing up for war.

She quickly composed a message to Jack, detailing what she had discovered. As she sent the message, she heard a noise behind her. Turning, she saw Dominic standing in the doorway, his expression a mix of suspicion and anger.

"What are you doing here, Rebecca?" he demanded, his voice cold.

Sarah's mind raced as she struggled to come up with a plausible explanation. "I was just checking the inventory," she lied. "Making sure everything is accounted for."

Dominic's eyes narrowed. "You're not supposed to be here. Get back to your post."

Sarah nodded and hurried out of the room, her heart pounding. She had narrowly avoided detection, but she knew her time was running out. She needed to get this information to Jack and Lisa before it was too late.

The next day, Jack and Lisa received Sarah's message and immediately mobilized their team. They coordinated with other law enforcement agencies, preparing for a raid on the syndicate's warehouse. The goal was to seize the weapons and apprehend as many members as possible.

As the raid commenced, Sarah found herself in the middle of a firefight. The warehouse erupted into chaos as law enforcement stormed in, guns blazing. She fought alongside her supposed comrades, maintaining her cover while secretly aiding the authorities.

Jack and Lisa led the charge, their determination evident as they moved through the warehouse, methodically clearing each room. They encountered fierce resistance, but their training and experience gave them the edge.

In the midst of the chaos, Sarah spotted Viktor. He was directing his men, his expression a mask of fury. She knew this was their chance to capture him, but it wouldn't be easy. Viktor was a formidable opponent, and his men were loyal to the death.

Sarah made her way to Jack and Lisa, her heart racing. "Viktor's in the back room. We need to move now."

They nodded, and together they pushed forward, fighting their way through the remaining syndicate members. The air was thick with smoke and the sound of gunfire, but they pressed on, their focus unwavering.

As they reached the back room, they found Viktor surrounded by his most trusted lieutenants. The tension was palpable as they prepared for the final confrontation.

"Viktor Ivanov," Jack called out, his voice steady. "It's over. Surrender now, and no one else has to die."

Viktor laughed, a cold, mirthless sound. "You think you can stop me? You're fools. This city is mine."

Jack and Lisa moved forward, their guns trained on Viktor. The room was a powder keg, ready to explode at any moment.

In a sudden burst of action, Viktor lunged at them, his gun raised. Jack fired, hitting him in the shoulder. Viktor stumbled, but didn't go down. He fired back, and the room erupted into chaos once more.

Sarah fought alongside Jack and Lisa, her training and instincts guiding her every move. The battle was fierce, but they managed to overpower Viktor's men, taking them down one by one.

As the dust settled, Viktor lay on the ground, wounded but alive. Jack and Lisa quickly secured him, their expressions grim.

"It's over, Viktor," Jack said, his voice filled with determination. "You're done."

Viktor glared at them, his eyes filled with hatred. "You think you've won? This is just the beginning. There are others like me. You can't stop us all."

"We'll see about that," Lisa replied, her voice resolute.

With Viktor in custody, the raid was deemed a success. The syndicate's operations had been dealt a significant blow, but Sarah knew the fight was far from over. The criminal underworld was vast and resilient, and there would always be new threats to face.

As they regrouped at the precinct, Jack and Lisa thanked Sarah for her bravery and dedication. She had risked everything to bring down the syndicate, and her efforts had paid off.

"You did good, Sarah," Jack said, his voice filled with pride. "We couldn't have done it without you."

Sarah smiled, though her heart was heavy. The battle had taken its toll, and she knew there would be more challenges ahead. But for now, she could take solace in the fact that they had made a difference.

As she left the precinct, Sarah looked out at the city she had fought so hard to protect. It was a city of contradictions, a place of beauty and darkness, hope and despair. But it was her city, and she was determined to keep fighting for it.

The road ahead was uncertain, and the dangers were ever-present. But Sarah knew that as long as there were people willing to stand up against the darkness, there was hope. And she would be there, fighting alongside them, for as long as it took.

The sun was setting over Bay City, casting a golden glow over the skyline. Sarah took a deep breath, feeling the weight of her journey. The battle against the crime syndicate was far from over, but she was ready for whatever came next.

With renewed determination, she walked into the twilight, ready to face the challenges that lay ahead. The fight for Bay City had only just begun, and Sarah Miller was prepared to see it through to the end.

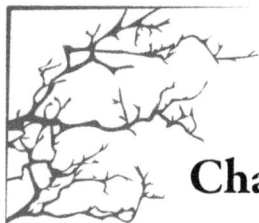

Chapter 4: The Money Trail

Detective Jack Thompson stared at the stacks of financial records piled high on his desk. The papers, covered in numbers and obscure transactions, represented a labyrinthine network of the syndicate's financial dealings. The sheer volume of data was daunting, but it was their best shot at dismantling the syndicate from within. Beside him, his partner, Detective Lisa Ramirez, methodically sifted through the documents, her brow furrowed in concentration.

Their investigation into the syndicate had led them to this point. The arrest of Viktor Ivanov, the syndicate's leader, had provided a wealth of information, but it was incomplete. To truly cripple the organization, they needed to follow the money.

"Look at this," Lisa said, pointing to a series of transactions. "These accounts are funneling money through a network of shell companies. It's classic money laundering."

Jack leaned over, scrutinizing the documents. "And here's the hub," he said, tracing a line to a name that stood out among the others: Emerald Cove Casino. "This place is the key. If we can connect the dots, we can bring down the whole operation."

Emerald Cove Casino was an open secret in Bay City. Located in a nondescript building on the outskirts of town, it was known to the underworld as a hub for illegal activities. Gambling, money laundering, drug deals – it all went down within its walls. But it was heavily guarded, and infiltrating it would be no small feat.

"We need a plan," Jack said, leaning back in his chair. "This place is a fortress. We can't just walk in there and start asking questions."

Lisa nodded. "We'll need to go undercover. Blend in, gather intelligence, and get out without blowing our cover."

Jack thought for a moment. "I know a guy who can get us in. We'll need to look the part, though. High rollers. People who belong."

Lisa smirked. "I think I can manage that."

The next evening, Jack and Lisa arrived at the Emerald Cove Casino, their appearances transformed. Jack wore a tailored suit, and Lisa donned a sleek evening gown. They looked every bit the part of wealthy gamblers, ready to throw money around. Their contact, a small-time crook named Benny, met them at the entrance.

"Benny," Jack said, shaking his hand. "Good to see you."

Benny was a wiry man with a nervous disposition. He glanced around, making sure they weren't being watched. "Jack, Lisa, you sure you want to do this? This place ain't no joke."

"We're sure," Lisa replied. "Just get us in, and we'll handle the rest."

Benny nodded, leading them through the opulent lobby and into the main casino floor. The room was a riot of color and sound – the clinking of chips, the whirl of roulette wheels, and the chatter of patrons. The air was thick with smoke and tension.

"Stay close to me," Benny said, guiding them to a high-stakes poker table. "This is where the big money moves."

Jack and Lisa took their seats, joining a group of well-dressed men and women who eyed them with curiosity. The dealer, a stone-faced man with a sharp gaze, dealt the cards with practiced precision.

As the game progressed, Jack and Lisa blended in seamlessly, playing their hands with skill and confidence. They kept their eyes and ears open, listening for any hint of the syndicate's activities. It wasn't long before they began to hear whispers.

"Did you hear about the shipment?" one man muttered to his companion. "Big score. Should keep the boss happy for a while."

"Yeah, but the cops are getting too close," the other replied. "We need to move fast."

Jack exchanged a glance with Lisa. They were on the right track.

Hours passed, and the tension in the room grew. Jack and Lisa had won and lost considerable sums of money, but their real focus was on the information they were gathering. They learned of a safe house used for storing cash and drugs, and of a major player named Lorenzo who was involved in the syndicate's financial operations.

As they prepared to leave, a commotion erupted near the bar. A burly man with a scar across his face was arguing with one of the casino's bouncers. The argument quickly escalated, and the man drew a gun.

"Get down!" Jack shouted, pulling Lisa to the floor as gunshots rang out. The casino erupted into chaos, with patrons scrambling for cover and security personnel rushing to subdue the shooter.

In the confusion, Jack and Lisa made their way toward the exit. They had just reached the door when a group of men blocked their path. The leader, a tall man with a cruel smile, looked them over.

"You're not leaving," he said, his voice cold. "We know who you are. Cops."

Jack and Lisa exchanged a quick glance. They had been made.

"What do we do?" Lisa whispered, her hand inching toward her concealed weapon.

"Follow my lead," Jack replied, his mind racing. "We need to create a distraction."

Jack lunged at the nearest man, catching him off guard and knocking him to the floor. Lisa drew her weapon, firing a shot into the ceiling to scatter the crowd. The room descended into chaos once more, and they used the confusion to their advantage.

They fought their way through the men, using every bit of their training and skill. Jack took down two with swift punches, while Lisa disarmed another and shoved him into a group of fleeing patrons. The path to the exit was clear, and they sprinted toward it, their hearts pounding.

Just as they reached the door, a bullet whizzed past Jack's head, narrowly missing him. He turned and saw the leader of the group raising his gun again. With no time to lose, Jack fired a shot, hitting the man in the leg and sending him crashing to the floor.

They burst through the exit and into the night, their breaths coming in ragged gasps. The alley behind the casino was dark and deserted, and they didn't stop running until they reached their car.

"Go, go, go!" Jack shouted as they jumped in, and Lisa floored the accelerator, sending the car speeding away from the casino.

They drove in silence, the adrenaline still coursing through their veins. It wasn't until they were several miles away that they finally spoke.

"That was too close," Lisa said, her voice shaking slightly.

Jack nodded, wiping sweat from his brow. "Yeah. But we got what we needed."

They returned to the precinct, where they reviewed the information they had gathered. The safe house, the shipment, and Lorenzo – it was all starting to come together. They had a lead on the syndicate's financial backbone, and they were determined to follow it to the end.

The next morning, they briefed Captain Reed on their findings. He listened intently, his expression grim.

"This is big," Reed said. "If we can take down their financial operations, we can cripple the entire organization."

"We need to move fast," Jack said. "The shipment is scheduled for tonight. We can hit the safe house and intercept it."

Reed nodded. "I'll assemble a team. This is our chance to strike a major blow."

That evening, Jack and Lisa led a team of officers to the safe house. It was a nondescript building in an industrial area, but they knew it was heavily guarded. As they approached, they could see men patrolling the perimeter, their faces hard and watchful.

"Stay sharp," Jack whispered to the team. "We go in fast and hard. No mistakes."

They moved in quickly, their weapons drawn. The first guards were taken out silently, but the element of surprise didn't last long. Soon, the air was filled with the sound of gunfire as the syndicate members fought back.

Jack and Lisa moved with precision, clearing room after room. They encountered fierce resistance, but their training and teamwork saw them through. Finally, they reached the main storage area, where they found stacks of cash and crates of drugs.

"Secure the area," Jack ordered, as officers moved to gather evidence. "We need to find Lorenzo."

They searched the building, but Lorenzo was nowhere to be found. It wasn't until they checked the basement that they discovered a hidden tunnel leading to a nearby warehouse.

"He must have escaped through here," Lisa said, her voice tense. "We need to follow him."

They entered the tunnel, moving quickly but cautiously. The air was damp and musty, and the walls were lined with old pipes and cables. It was a claustrophobic space, but they pressed on, determined to catch Lorenzo.

The tunnel led to a large warehouse, filled with more crates and equipment. They spread out, searching for any sign of their target. It wasn't long before they found him, hiding behind a stack of crates, a gun in his hand.

"Lorenzo, drop the weapon!" Jack shouted, his voice echoing through the cavernous space.

Lorenzo hesitated, his eyes darting around as if looking for an escape route. But he was cornered, and he knew it.

"Alright, alright," he said, tossing the gun aside. "Don't shoot."

Jack and Lisa moved in, cuffing him and leading him out of the warehouse. As they did, Jack couldn't help but feel a sense of satisfaction. They had struck a major blow against the syndicate, and Lorenzo's capture would provide valuable information.

Back at the precinct, Lorenzo was interrogated. He was reluctant to talk at first, but the weight of the evidence against him and the promise of a reduced sentence eventually loosened his tongue.

"I handle the money," Lorenzo admitted. "I launder it through the casino and other businesses. But there's more. The syndicate is planning something big, something that'll make Helms' assassination look like child's play."

Jack leaned forward, his eyes intense. "What are they planning?"

Lorenzo hesitated, glancing around nervously. "It's an attack. On the city's power grid. They're going to knock out the electricity and create chaos. It's happening in two days."

Jack and Lisa exchanged a shocked glance. The implications were staggering. If the syndicate succeeded, the city would be plunged into darkness, and the resulting chaos would be catastrophic.

"We need to stop this," Lisa said, her voice urgent. "We have to shut down their operation and secure the power grid."

Reed agreed, and plans were quickly set in motion. They coordinated with the city's utility company, law enforcement agencies, and even the National Guard. It was an all-hands-on-deck operation, and failure was not an option.

The day of the planned attack dawned, and the city was on high alert. Officers were stationed at key points around the power grid, and teams were ready to respond at a moment's notice. Jack and Lisa led the operation, their determination unwavering.

As night fell, they received word that syndicate members were moving into position. The tension was palpable as they waited for the signal to move. When it finally came, they sprang into action, converging on the syndicate's target locations.

The ensuing battle was fierce. The syndicate had brought in heavily armed men, and they fought with the desperation of those who knew they were facing the end. But the coordinated efforts of law enforcement and the National Guard proved too much for them.

Jack and Lisa fought side by side, their movements fluid and synchronized. They cleared buildings, disarmed bombs, and apprehended suspects. The operation was a success, and the power grid was secured.

In the aftermath, they stood together, surveying the scene. The syndicate had been dealt a crippling blow, and the city was safe – for now.

"We did it," Lisa said, her voice filled with relief.

"Yeah," Jack replied, his eyes scanning the horizon. "But this isn't the end. There will always be new threats, new enemies. We have to stay vigilant."

As they returned to the precinct, exhausted but triumphant, Jack couldn't help but feel a sense of pride. They had followed the money trail, faced incredible danger, and emerged victorious. The fight against the syndicate was far from over, but they had made significant progress.

In the days that followed, they continued to dismantle the syndicate's operations, using the information gathered from Lorenzo and other captured members. The network of crime and corruption was vast, but piece by piece, they were tearing it apart.

As the sun set over Bay City, Jack and Lisa sat in their office, surrounded by files and evidence. The work was never-ending, but they were ready for whatever came next. They had faced the darkness and emerged stronger, and they would continue to fight for justice.

The city was a better place because of their efforts, and they were determined to keep it that way. The road ahead was long and fraught with challenges, but they were ready to face it together. The fight for Bay City had only just begun, and Jack and Lisa were prepared to see it through to the end.

Chapter 5: Shadows of the Past

Detective Jack Thompson sat in his dimly lit apartment, staring at an old, weathered photograph in his hands. The edges were frayed, and the image had faded with time, but the faces in the picture were still clear. It was a photo of him and his younger brother, Michael, taken many years ago. Michael's smile was wide and carefree, a stark contrast to the serious expression Jack wore even then.

Jack's thoughts drifted back to the past, to the days when he and Michael had been inseparable. They had grown up in a rough neighborhood, where crime was a part of everyday life. Their father had been a cop, a good man who believed in justice and had instilled those values in his sons. But their father had died in the line of duty when they were still young, leaving their mother to raise them alone.

The loss had hit Jack hard. He had idolized his father, and his death had left a void that nothing could fill. Jack had vowed to follow in his father's footsteps, to become a cop and fight the crime that had taken his father from him. Michael, on the other hand, had taken a different path. The pain of their father's death had driven him into the arms of the very underworld their father had fought against.

Jack's mind wandered to the day that had changed everything. It had been a rainy afternoon, the kind of day that seemed to wash away the world's colors, leaving everything gray and lifeless. Jack had been a rookie cop then, fresh out of the academy and full of idealism. He had been on patrol with his partner, a grizzled veteran named Ray who had taken him under his wing.

They had received a call about a drug deal going down in an abandoned warehouse. When they arrived, the scene was chaotic. Gunshots rang out, and Jack had felt the adrenaline surge through his veins. He and Ray had moved in, trying to secure the area. In the midst of the chaos, Jack had spotted a familiar face – his brother, Michael.

Michael had been standing with a group of men, all heavily armed. Their eyes had met, and for a brief moment, time had seemed to stand still. Jack had felt a surge of hope that maybe, just maybe, he could save his brother. But then, Michael had raised his gun and pointed it at Jack. The look in his eyes was one of desperation and anger.

"Michael, don't!" Jack had shouted, his voice filled with a mix of fear and determination.

But it had been too late. A shot had rung out, and Ray had fallen to the ground, clutching his chest. Jack had fired back, hitting one of the men with Michael. In the ensuing chaos, Michael had fled, disappearing into the shadows.

Ray had died in Jack's arms that day, another good man lost to the violence that plagued their city. The guilt had eaten at Jack, gnawing at his soul. He had lost his partner, his mentor, and his brother all in one day. From that moment on, Jack had vowed to dismantle the crime syndicate that had taken so much from him.

The years that followed had been a blur of investigations, arrests, and near misses. Jack had risen through the ranks, earning a reputation as a relentless and determined detective. But the pain of his past never left him. It was a constant shadow, a reminder of the personal cost of his crusade against organized crime.

As Jack sat in his apartment, lost in memories, his phone buzzed. It was a message from Lisa. "Need to meet. Urgent."

Jack put the photograph back in the drawer and headed out, his mind still lingering on the past. He met Lisa at a small diner, a place they often used for clandestine meetings. She was already there, her expression serious.

"Jack, we've got a lead," she said, sliding a file across the table.

Jack opened the file and scanned the contents. It detailed the activities of a man named Alexei Petrov, a high-ranking member of the syndicate. Alexei had been involved in some of the syndicate's most lucrative operations, and his capture could provide crucial information.

"We believe he's connected to the shipment we intercepted," Lisa continued. "And there's more. He's got ties to Michael."

Jack's heart skipped a beat. "Michael? How?"

"Michael worked for Alexei for a while. We've got informants who say he was close to him, part of his inner circle. If we can get to Alexei, we might be able to find out what happened to Michael."

Jack's mind raced. He hadn't seen or heard from Michael since that fateful day at the warehouse. The thought of his brother being involved with someone as dangerous as Alexei was both infuriating and heartbreaking.

"We need to bring Alexei in," Jack said, his voice steady. "Where is he?"

Lisa hesitated. "We've tracked him to a safe house in the Southside. But it's heavily guarded. We'll need to be careful."

Jack nodded. "Let's do it. The sooner we get him, the better."

That night, they assembled a team and moved in on the safe house. The air was thick with tension as they approached, their movements silent and coordinated. Jack's heart pounded in his chest, a mix of adrenaline and anxiety.

They breached the building, and chaos erupted. Gunfire echoed through the halls as they engaged the guards. Jack and Lisa moved with precision, clearing room after room. Finally, they reached a reinforced door at the end of a corridor.

"This has to be it," Jack said, his voice barely a whisper.

They breached the door and found Alexei inside, flanked by two heavily armed men. The room was filled with stacks of cash and documents – evidence of the syndicate's operations.

"Drop your weapons!" Jack shouted, his gun trained on Alexei.

Alexei smirked, but he complied, raising his hands in surrender. His men followed suit, and the team moved in to secure them.

"Alexei Petrov, you're under arrest," Lisa said, cuffing him.

As they led Alexei out, Jack couldn't help but feel a sense of satisfaction. They had captured a key figure in the syndicate, and with him, the potential to uncover the truth about Michael.

Back at the precinct, Alexei was interrogated. He was defiant at first, but Jack's relentless questioning began to wear him down. Finally, he spoke.

"Michael... he was like a brother to me," Alexei said, his voice tinged with a hint of nostalgia. "But he got in too deep. He couldn't handle the pressure."

"What happened to him?" Jack demanded.

Alexei sighed. "He tried to get out. Wanted to leave the life behind. But the syndicate doesn't let go that easily. They sent men after him. I tried to warn him, but he didn't listen."

Jack's heart sank. "Is he dead?"

"I don't know," Alexei admitted. "Last I heard, he was hiding out in the East End. But that was months ago. He could be anywhere now."

Jack clenched his fists, the anger and frustration boiling inside him. Michael had tried to escape, but the syndicate had dragged him back in. It was a painful reminder of the hold they had over so many lives.

"We need to find him," Jack said, his voice determined. "I can't let him disappear again."

Lisa nodded. "We'll do everything we can. But for now, we need to focus on Alexei. He's our key to dismantling the syndicate."

They spent the next few days going through the evidence they had collected. The documents from Alexei's safe house provided a wealth of information – bank records, transaction logs, and names of key players. It was a tangled web, but Jack and Lisa were determined to unravel it.

As they worked, Jack couldn't shake the memories of his past. Flashbacks of his early career, the days when he had been filled with hope and determination, haunted him. He remembered the long nights, the endless stakeouts, and the moments of doubt. But he also remembered the camaraderie, the victories, and the sense of purpose.

One memory stood out above the rest. It was a case from his rookie years, a brutal murder that had shocked the city. The victim had been a young woman, innocent and full of life. The investigation had led Jack into the heart of the syndicate's operations, and it was there that he had first encountered Viktor Ivanov.

Viktor had been a rising star in the underworld, his influence growing with each passing day. Jack had pursued him relentlessly, but Viktor had always been one step ahead. The case had ended in a stalemate, with Viktor slipping through Jack's fingers. But it had ignited a fire in Jack, a burning desire to bring Viktor to justice.

Years later, that fire still burned. The arrest of Viktor had been a significant victory, but Jack knew it was just the beginning. The syndicate was vast, and its roots ran deep. To truly dismantle it, they needed to cut off its financial lifeline and take down its key players.

As Jack poured over the documents, he found a name that stood out – Ivan Romanov. Ivan was a powerful figure in the syndicate, responsible for managing their finances and laundering money. He was known to be ruthless and cunning, a man who would stop at nothing to protect his interests.

"We need to go after Romanov," Jack said, showing Lisa the file. "He's the one pulling the strings behind the scenes."

Lisa nodded. "Agreed. But he's elusive. We'll need to be smart about this."

They began to dig deeper into Romanov's activities, tracing his connections and financial dealings. It was a painstaking process, but they made progress. They discovered that Romanov had been using a network of offshore accounts to launder money, funneling it through legitimate businesses to cover his tracks.

One of these businesses was a high-end nightclub in the downtown area. It was a front for the syndicate's operations, a place where deals were made, and money changed hands. Jack and Lisa decided to investigate, hoping to gather evidence that would lead them to Romanov.

They arrived at the nightclub late one evening, dressed in casual attire to blend in. The place was packed, the music loud and the lights dim. They moved through the crowd, keeping a low profile as they surveyed the scene.

Jack's eyes were drawn to a group of men sitting in a VIP section. They were well-dressed and appeared to be deep in conversation. Jack recognized one of them from the files – a man named Sergei, one of Romanov's lieutenants.

"Over there," Jack said, nodding towards the group. "That's Sergei. He's connected to Romanov."

Lisa nodded. "Let's get closer. See if we can hear anything."

They moved towards the VIP section, staying just out of sight. As they listened, they caught snippets of the conversation.

"...shipment coming in next week... Romanov wants it handled discreetly..."

"...new contacts in the East End... need to keep the heat off..."

Jack's heart raced. This was the break they needed. If they could intercept the shipment and gather evidence, they could build a case against Romanov.

They continued to listen, but their presence didn't go unnoticed. One of Sergei's men spotted them and alerted the others. Sergei's eyes narrowed as he looked in their direction.

"Time to go," Jack whispered to Lisa.

They began to move away, but Sergei's men were quick. They followed Jack and Lisa through the crowd, closing in on them. Jack and Lisa picked up the pace, heading for the exit.

As they reached the door, Sergei's men confronted them. "Where do you think you're going?"

Jack's mind raced. They were outnumbered and outgunned, but he wasn't about to back down. "Just leaving. No need for trouble."

One of the men sneered. "Too late for that."

A fight broke out, and the nightclub erupted into chaos. Jack and Lisa fought back, using their training and instincts to defend themselves. The bouncers moved in to break up the fight, and in the confusion, Jack and Lisa managed to slip away.

They raced through the streets, adrenaline pumping, until they were sure they were no longer being followed. They stopped to catch their breath, their minds still reeling from the encounter.

"That was close," Lisa said, her voice shaky.

"Too close," Jack agreed. "But we got what we needed. Romanov's planning a shipment. We need to intercept it."

The next few days were a whirlwind of activity as they coordinated with other law enforcement agencies. They set up surveillance on the nightclub and tracked Sergei's movements, gathering as much information as they could.

Finally, the night of the shipment arrived. They had pinpointed the location – a warehouse on the docks. Jack and Lisa led the operation, moving in with a team of officers.

The warehouse was dimly lit, the air thick with the smell of salt and oil. They moved silently, their weapons drawn, as they approached the building. Inside, they could hear voices and the sound of machinery.

They breached the warehouse, and chaos erupted. The syndicate's men fought back fiercely, but Jack and Lisa were relentless. They moved through the building, clearing each room and securing the area.

In the main storage area, they found the shipment – crates of weapons and drugs, ready to be distributed. It was a significant victory, and the evidence they gathered would be crucial in building their case against Romanov.

But the victory was bittersweet. As they secured the area, Jack's thoughts turned to Michael. He still didn't know what had happened to his brother, and the uncertainty gnawed at him.

Back at the precinct, they reviewed the evidence and prepared their case. They had enough to take down Romanov, but Jack knew it was just one piece of the puzzle. The syndicate was vast, and there were still many battles to be fought.

As he sat in his office, his thoughts drifted back to his father and the values he had instilled in him. The fight for justice, the pursuit of truth – it was a legacy Jack was determined to uphold. His father had given his life for those values, and Jack was prepared to do the same.

The memories of his early career, the personal losses, and the painful choices he had made all served to strengthen his resolve. The shadows of the past were ever-present, but they also guided him, reminding him of what was at stake.

The road ahead was long and fraught with challenges, but Jack was ready. He had faced the darkness before and emerged stronger. The fight against the syndicate was far from over, but he knew he wasn't alone. He had Lisa by his side, and together, they would continue the battle.

As the sun set over Bay City, casting a golden glow over the skyline, Jack felt a renewed sense of purpose. The shadows of the past would always be with him, but they would not define him. He was a fighter, a protector, and he would not rest until the city was free from the grip of the syndicate.

The fight for Bay City had only just begun, and Jack Thompson was prepared to see it through to the end.

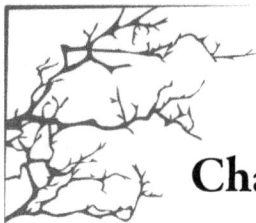

Chapter 6: Betrayal Within

Detective Sarah Miller sat in her small apartment, the flickering glow of her laptop screen the only source of light in the room. She was deep in thought, reviewing the latest intelligence reports she had received from her contacts within the syndicate. Something wasn't adding up. Over the past few weeks, the syndicate had seemed to be one step ahead of every operation Jack and Lisa had planned. It was as if someone was feeding them information.

The possibility that there was a mole within the police department was becoming increasingly hard to ignore. Sarah had joined the department with a singular mission: to bring down the crime syndicate that had a stranglehold on Bay City. She had gone deep undercover, risking her life to gather intelligence and infiltrate their operations. Now, all her hard work seemed to be unraveling.

Sarah decided it was time to voice her concerns to Jack and Lisa. She needed their help to uncover the traitor and prevent further leaks. The stakes were too high to ignore this threat any longer.

The next morning, Sarah met Jack and Lisa at their usual spot, a quiet coffee shop away from the prying eyes of their colleagues. The tension in the air was palpable as they sat down at a corner table, their expressions serious.

"I've been going over the recent intel," Sarah began, her voice low. "And I think we have a mole within the department. Someone's been leaking our plans to the syndicate."

Jack's eyes narrowed. "You're sure?"

Sarah nodded. "It's the only explanation. Every time we plan an operation, the syndicate seems to be prepared. They're always one step ahead of us."

Lisa frowned, her mind racing. "This is bad. If there's a mole, it means we can't trust anyone. We need to figure out who it is and fast."

Jack leaned back in his chair, his expression thoughtful. "We need to be careful. If we start accusing people without solid evidence, it could backfire. We need to catch the mole in the act."

Sarah agreed. "I have an idea. We could feed false information to a small group of people and see if it gets back to the syndicate. It's risky, but it might be our best shot at uncovering the traitor."

Lisa nodded. "It's a good plan. We just need to make sure the information we use is believable enough to draw them out."

Jack looked at Sarah, his eyes filled with determination. "Let's do it. We'll start by narrowing down our suspects and then set the trap."

They spent the next few hours going over their list of suspects, carefully selecting those who had access to sensitive information. It was a delicate process, and the weight of their task hung heavily over them. They couldn't afford to make a mistake.

Once they had their list, they crafted a piece of false intelligence. It was a plausible but entirely fabricated plan to raid one of the syndicate's safe houses. They would monitor the suspects closely, looking for any sign that the information had been leaked.

The following days were a blur of tension and suspicion. Jack, Lisa, and Sarah kept a close eye on their suspects, watching for any unusual behavior. The pressure was immense, and the atmosphere within the department was charged with unease.

Finally, their patience paid off. One of the suspects, Officer James Collins, began acting strangely. He was seen making secretive phone calls and meeting with individuals outside of his usual circles. Jack and Lisa decided to follow him, hoping to catch him in the act.

One evening, they trailed Collins to a rundown bar on the outskirts of the city. The place was a known hangout for low-level criminals, and it was the perfect spot for a clandestine meeting. Jack and Lisa watched from a distance as Collins entered the bar and took a seat in a secluded corner.

A few minutes later, a man approached Collins and sat down across from him. Jack recognized the man as one of the syndicate's known associates. His heart pounded as he realized they were on the verge of uncovering the mole.

They couldn't hear the conversation, but the body language spoke volumes. Collins was nervous, glancing around the bar as he spoke. The syndicate associate listened intently, occasionally nodding in agreement. After a few minutes, they exchanged something – a small envelope – and then parted ways.

Jack and Lisa followed Collins as he left the bar and headed back towards the city. They maintained a safe distance, ensuring they weren't detected. Collins led them to a secluded alleyway where he met with another man. This time, it was someone higher up in the syndicate, a man known as Victor Morales.

The conversation was brief, and Collins handed over the envelope he had received at the bar. Victor pocketed it and then walked away, leaving Collins alone in the alley. Jack and Lisa watched as Collins hurried back to his car and drove off.

"This is it," Jack said, his voice filled with a mix of anger and determination. "We've got our mole."

They returned to the precinct, where they shared their findings with Sarah. The betrayal cut deep, and the realization that one of their own had been working with the syndicate was a bitter pill to swallow.

"We need to bring him in," Lisa said, her voice cold. "He needs to answer for what he's done."

Jack nodded. "Agreed. But we need to handle this carefully. If Collins realizes we're onto him, he might run."

They devised a plan to apprehend Collins without arousing suspicion. The next morning, Jack and Lisa approached him at his desk, their expressions neutral.

"Collins, we need to talk," Jack said, his tone firm.

Collins looked up, his eyes widening in surprise. "Sure, what's this about?"

"Just a routine debrief," Lisa replied smoothly. "Come with us."

They led Collins to an interrogation room, where Sarah was waiting. As soon as the door closed, Jack and Lisa moved to block the exit, their expressions hardening.

"Collins, we know you've been working with the syndicate," Jack said, his voice filled with barely controlled anger. "We've got you on tape meeting with their associates. There's no point in denying it."

Collins' face went pale, and he glanced around the room, realizing there was no escape. "I... I can explain..."

"Save it," Lisa snapped. "You've been betraying us, compromising our operations, putting all our lives at risk. You're going to answer for this."

Collins slumped in his chair, defeated. "Okay, okay. I'll talk. Just... don't hurt me."

Sarah leaned forward, her eyes cold. "Start from the beginning. How did you get involved with the syndicate?"

Collins took a deep breath, his voice trembling as he began to speak. "It started a few years ago. I got into some trouble – gambling debts, bad decisions. The syndicate offered to help me out, pay off my debts. In return, I had to feed them information."

"And you went along with it," Jack said, his voice filled with contempt. "You sold us out for money."

Collins nodded miserably. "I didn't have a choice. They threatened my family. I couldn't risk it."

"What else have you told them?" Lisa demanded. "We need to know everything."

Collins hesitated, then began to list the operations he had compromised, the plans he had leaked. It was a long list, and each revelation stung like a fresh wound.

When he was finished, Jack looked at Sarah. "We need to take this to the captain. Collins needs to be formally charged."

Sarah nodded. "Agreed. We'll make sure he faces justice."

They left Collins in the interrogation room and went to see Captain Reed. The captain's face hardened as he listened to their report.

"This is a serious breach," Reed said, his voice low. "We'll handle it internally for now, but we need to make sure Collins doesn't get the chance to escape."

They moved quickly to secure Collins, placing him under guard and beginning the process of gathering evidence for his trial. The betrayal had shaken them, but they knew they couldn't let it derail their mission.

As the days passed, the full extent of the syndicate's reach and influence became alarmingly evident. The information Collins had provided revealed a network of corruption that extended far beyond the police department. Judges, politicians, business leaders – all had been compromised by the syndicate's web of influence.

Jack and Lisa knew they had to act swiftly to dismantle this network. They began to build a case, using the evidence they had gathered from Collins and their own investigations. It was a monumental task, but they were determined to see it through.

One evening, as they worked late in the precinct, Jack received a call from Sarah. "We've got a lead on another key figure in the syndicate," she said. "A man named Martin Delgado. He's been handling their political connections."

"Where can we find him?" Jack asked.

"He's meeting with one of his contacts tonight at a hotel downtown," Sarah replied. "I'll send you the details."

Jack and Lisa quickly gathered their gear and headed to the hotel. The building was a luxurious high-rise, frequented by the city's elite. They moved quietly through the lobby, keeping a low profile as they made their way to the meeting room.

As they approached, they could hear voices inside. Jack signaled for Lisa to take the lead, and they burst into the room, their weapons drawn.

Martin Delgado was sitting at a table with a man Jack recognized as a prominent city council member. The two men looked up in shock as Jack and Lisa entered.

"Hands where we can see them," Lisa ordered, her voice steady.

Delgado and the council member raised their hands, their expressions filled with fear. Jack moved forward and cuffed them, securing the room.

"You're making a big mistake," Delgado said, his voice shaking. "You don't know who you're dealing with."

Jack ignored him, his focus on gathering evidence. They searched the room and found documents detailing the syndicate's political connections, proof of bribes and corruption that reached the highest levels of the city's government.

Back at the precinct, they began to compile the evidence, building a case that would expose the full extent of the syndicate's influence. It was a daunting task, but they knew it was their best shot at bringing the entire operation down.

As the days turned into weeks, the tension within the department remained high. The discovery of the mole had created an atmosphere of suspicion and mistrust. But Jack, Lisa, and Sarah pushed forward, their resolve unwavering.

One night, as they worked late in the precinct, they received an unexpected visit. Captain Reed entered the room, his expression grave.

"We've just received word that the syndicate is planning a major attack," Reed said. "They're targeting a public event – the mayor's re-election rally."

Jack's heart sank. The rally was scheduled for the next day, and it would be attended by thousands of people. The potential for casualties was enormous.

"We need to move fast," Lisa said, her voice filled with urgency. "We can't let this happen."

They quickly devised a plan to secure the rally and intercept the syndicate's operatives. It was a high-risk operation, but they had no choice.

The next day, they arrived at the rally early, coordinating with other law enforcement agencies to set up security. The atmosphere was tense as they prepared for the worst.

As the rally began, Jack and Lisa moved through the crowd, their eyes scanning for any sign of trouble. The mayor took the stage, and the crowd erupted in applause.

Suddenly, Jack spotted a man moving through the crowd, his behavior suspicious. He nudged Lisa, and they moved to intercept him.

"Stop right there!" Jack shouted, drawing his weapon.

The man turned, his eyes wide with fear, and began to run. Jack and Lisa gave chase, their hearts pounding as they navigated the crowded plaza.

The chase led them to a nearby alley, where the man stumbled and fell. Jack quickly apprehended him, and they found a small device in his pocket – a remote detonator.

"We've got him," Jack said, his voice filled with relief. "But we need to find the bomb."

They worked quickly, coordinating with the bomb squad to locate and disarm the device. It was hidden under the stage, a crude but powerful explosive that could have caused massive devastation.

As the bomb squad disarmed the device, the reality of what they had prevented sank in. They had narrowly averted a tragedy, and the syndicate's plan had been foiled.

Back at the precinct, they reflected on the events of the past weeks. The betrayal, the investigations, the near-miss at the rally – it had all taken a toll. But they had emerged stronger, their resolve to bring down the syndicate unwavering.

Jack looked at Lisa and Sarah, his expression filled with determination. "We've made progress, but we can't let our guard down. The syndicate is still out there, and they're not going to give up easily."

Lisa nodded. "Agreed. We need to stay vigilant and keep pushing forward."

Sarah smiled, her eyes filled with determination. "We've come this far. We're not stopping now."

As they continued their work, the shadows of betrayal and corruption loomed large. But Jack, Lisa, and Sarah knew they had the strength and resolve to face whatever challenges lay ahead. The fight for Bay City was far from over, but they were ready to see it through to the end.

The city's future depended on their efforts, and they were determined to make a difference. The battle against the syndicate was a long and arduous one, but with each victory, they moved one step closer to reclaiming their city.

As the sun set over Bay City, casting a golden glow over the skyline, Jack felt a renewed sense of purpose. The shadows of betrayal had only strengthened his resolve, and he knew that together, they could overcome any obstacle.

The fight for Bay City had only just begun, and Jack Thompson was prepared to see it through to the end. With Lisa and Sarah by his side, he knew they could face whatever challenges lay ahead and emerge victorious. The future of Bay City was in their hands, and they would not rest until it was safe once more.

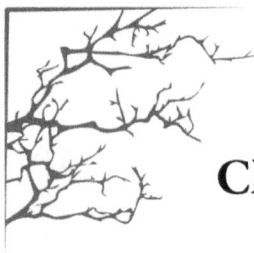

Chapter 7: The Hitman's Code

The night was cold and unyielding, a perfect backdrop for Viktor Petrov's line of work. He moved through the shadows with a practiced ease, his movements fluid and precise. Viktor was a hitman, one of the best in the business, and his services were highly sought after by those who needed a problem eliminated with ruthless efficiency. His current employer was the crime syndicate that had Bay City in its grip, and Viktor's latest assignment was one that came with high stakes and even higher risks.

Viktor had been born into a world of violence and chaos. Growing up in the war-torn streets of Eastern Europe, he had learned early on that survival meant being stronger, smarter, and more ruthless than those around him. He had been a soldier, a mercenary, and eventually, a hitman. It was a natural progression, and one that suited him well. But despite the blood on his hands, Viktor had a code of ethics, a set of rules that guided his actions and kept him grounded in a world of darkness.

His latest target was Detective Jack Thompson, a relentless cop who had been making life difficult for the syndicate. Jack and his partner, Detective Lisa Ramirez, had been closing in on the syndicate's operations, dismantling their networks and bringing their key players to justice. The syndicate had decided that Jack needed to be eliminated, and they had turned to Viktor to get the job done.

Viktor stood on the rooftop of a building overlooking the precinct where Jack and Lisa worked. He watched through the scope of his sniper rifle, his breath steady and his focus unwavering. He had spent weeks studying Jack's movements, learning his routines and habits. Tonight was the night he would make his move.

As he waited for the perfect moment, Viktor's mind drifted back to the events that had led him to this point. He had always prided himself on being a professional, someone who did his job with precision and detachment. But lately, he had begun to question the path he was on. The faces of his victims haunted his dreams, and the weight of his actions pressed heavily on his conscience.

Despite his internal conflict, Viktor remained committed to his code. He only took contracts on those who were guilty, those who had chosen a life of crime and corruption. It was a small consolation, but it was enough to keep him going. Jack, however, was different. He was a cop, a man who had dedicated his life to fighting the very evil that Viktor perpetuated. It was a line Viktor had never crossed before, and the thought of doing so filled him with unease.

As he watched Jack and Lisa exit the precinct, Viktor's finger tightened on the trigger. He had a clear shot, and the conditions were perfect. But something held him back. He hesitated, the weight of his conscience battling with his professional instincts. In that moment of hesitation, he saw something in Jack's eyes – a determination, a fire that mirrored his own. It was enough to make Viktor question everything.

Before he could make a decision, a noise behind him shattered his concentration. He spun around, his gun at the ready, but it was too late. A figure emerged from the shadows, a man with a gun aimed directly at him.

"Viktor Petrov," the man said, his voice cold and calculating. "The syndicate has decided you're a liability."

Viktor recognized the man – Anton, a rival hitman who had always resented Viktor's reputation. The realization hit him like a punch to the gut. The syndicate had turned on him, and he was now the target.

Without a moment's hesitation, Viktor lunged at Anton, their guns clashing as they grappled on the rooftop. The fight was brutal and intense, both men skilled and determined. But Viktor's experience gave him the edge, and he managed to disarm Anton and knock him to the ground.

"Why?" Viktor demanded, his voice filled with anger and betrayal.

"The syndicate doesn't trust you anymore," Anton spat. "You've been questioning your orders, hesitating. They think you're a risk."

Viktor's mind raced. He knew he couldn't stay here, couldn't continue working for an organization that had marked him for death. He had to disappear, had to find a way to protect himself and those he cared about. And that meant he needed to warn Jack and Lisa.

Leaving Anton unconscious on the rooftop, Viktor made his way down the fire escape and into the shadows of the city. He knew he couldn't go to the precinct directly – the syndicate's reach was too extensive. Instead, he decided to leave a message, a warning that would alert Jack and Lisa to the danger they were in.

He made his way to a nearby alley, where he found an old, abandoned payphone. He dialed the precinct's main line, disguising his voice as best he could.

"Detective Thompson," he said when Jack answered. "This is a warning. The syndicate has put a hit on you and your partner. You need to be careful. Trust no one."

Jack's voice was filled with suspicion and confusion. "Who is this? How do you know?"

"Just a concerned citizen," Viktor replied before hanging up.

As he left the alley, Viktor knew he had made the right decision. He couldn't continue living a life of violence and betrayal. He had to find a way to make amends, to find some semblance of redemption. And that meant he needed to bring down the syndicate, once and for all.

Jack sat at his desk, staring at the phone in disbelief. The call had been brief, but the message was clear. Someone was targeting him and Lisa, and they needed to be on their guard. He quickly called Lisa over, explaining the situation.

"We need to figure out who made that call," Lisa said, her eyes filled with concern. "And we need to tighten security around the precinct."

Jack nodded. "Agreed. But we also need to keep investigating the syndicate. If they're targeting us, it means we're getting close."

They spent the next few days on high alert, constantly watching their backs and questioning everyone around them. The tension was palpable, and the stress of the situation began to take its toll. But Jack and Lisa were determined to press on, to continue their fight against the syndicate.

As they delved deeper into their investigation, they uncovered more evidence of the syndicate's operations. They learned of a new shipment of weapons coming into the city, a deal that could give them the leverage they needed to strike a decisive blow. But they also knew that the syndicate would be watching, waiting for any opportunity to eliminate them.

One evening, as they prepared to raid the location of the shipment, they received an unexpected visitor. Viktor appeared at the precinct, his face bruised and his clothes disheveled. He looked like a man on the run, a man with nothing left to lose.

"Detective Thompson, Detective Ramirez," he said, his voice filled with urgency. "I need to talk to you."

Jack and Lisa exchanged a wary glance. They recognized Viktor from their files – a hitman with a deadly reputation. But there was something different about him now, a desperation that spoke to a deeper truth.

"Why should we trust you?" Jack asked, his voice cautious.

"Because I'm your only chance," Viktor replied. "The syndicate has put a hit on you, and they're not going to stop until you're dead. But I can help you. I know their operations, their plans. Together, we can bring them down."

Lisa studied Viktor, her eyes searching for any sign of deceit. "Why should we believe you? You're a killer, a man who's done unspeakable things."

Viktor's expression hardened. "I know what I am. But I also know that I can't keep living this way. The syndicate has turned on me, and I'm done with them. I want to make things right, to find some redemption. And that starts with helping you."

Jack and Lisa exchanged another glance, their minds racing. They knew they were taking a risk, but they also knew that Viktor could provide them with invaluable information.

"Alright," Jack said finally. "We'll work together. But you step out of line, and you're done. Got it?"

Viktor nodded. "Got it."

They spent the next few hours going over their plan, with Viktor providing crucial insights into the syndicate's operations. He told them about the shipment, the security measures in place, and the key players involved. It was a dangerous mission, but they were determined to see it through.

As they prepared to move out, Viktor pulled Jack aside. "There's something else you need to know. The syndicate has a mole within your department. That's how they knew about your plans."

Jack's eyes widened in shock. "Who?"

Viktor hesitated. "I don't know. But I have a feeling we'll find out soon enough."

With that ominous warning hanging over them, they set out for the location of the shipment. The night was dark and foreboding, the air thick with anticipation. They moved quietly, their senses on high alert, as they approached the warehouse where the deal was going down.

The warehouse was heavily guarded, with armed men patrolling the perimeter. Viktor led the way, his knowledge of the syndicate's operations guiding them through the shadows. They moved with precision, taking out the guards silently and efficiently.

As they entered the warehouse, they could hear the sounds of voices and the clinking of weapons. The syndicate members were busy preparing the shipment, unaware of the danger lurking in the shadows.

Jack and Lisa signaled their team, and they moved in, guns drawn. The room erupted into chaos as the syndicate members realized they were under attack. Gunfire echoed through the warehouse, and the air was filled with the acrid smell of smoke and gunpowder.

Viktor fought alongside Jack and Lisa, his skills as a hitman proving invaluable. He moved with lethal precision, taking down the syndicate members with ease. But the fight was far from over.

In the midst of the chaos, a familiar figure emerged – Anton, the rival hitman who had tried to kill Viktor. He was flanked by a group of heavily armed men, and his eyes were filled with cold determination.

"Viktor," Anton sneered. "I should have finished you off when I had the chance."

Viktor's expression hardened. "This ends now, Anton."

The two men faced off, their guns aimed at each other. The tension in the room was palpable as they stared each other down, the fate of the battle hanging in the balance.

Without warning, Anton fired, and Viktor dove to the side, narrowly avoiding the bullet. The room erupted into chaos once more as the two hitmen engaged in a deadly dance of bullets and blades.

Jack and Lisa fought their way through the chaos, their focus on securing the shipment and taking down the syndicate members. But their eyes were also on Viktor, watching as he faced off against Anton.

The fight was brutal and intense, both men skilled and determined. But Viktor's experience gave him the edge, and he managed to disarm Anton and knock him to the ground.

"It's over, Anton," Viktor said, his voice filled with finality.

Anton glared up at him, his eyes filled with hatred. "You may have won this round, Viktor. But the syndicate won't stop. They'll keep coming for you, and for them."

Viktor's expression remained steely. "Let them come. I'm ready."

With Anton defeated and the shipment secured, Jack and Lisa moved quickly to gather evidence and apprehend the remaining syndicate members. The operation had been a success, but they knew the fight was far from over.

Back at the precinct, they debriefed Viktor, going over the details of the operation and the information he had provided. The betrayal within their ranks weighed heavily on their minds, and they knew they needed to root out the mole before the syndicate struck again.

"Do you have any leads on who the mole might be?" Jack asked Viktor.

Viktor shook his head. "No. But I know they're close to the top. Someone with access to sensitive information."

Jack and Lisa exchanged a worried glance. The realization that someone within their own department was working against them was a bitter pill to swallow.

"We'll find them," Lisa said, her voice filled with determination. "And when we do, they'll face justice."

Viktor nodded. "In the meantime, we need to keep the pressure on the syndicate. They're reeling from this setback, and we need to capitalize on it."

Over the next few weeks, they continued their investigation, using the information Viktor provided to dismantle the syndicate's operations piece by piece. The tension within the department remained high, with everyone on edge and suspicious of each other.

Finally, their efforts paid off. They discovered that the mole was none other than Captain Reed, the man who had been overseeing their investigation. The betrayal cut deep, and the realization that their trusted leader had been working with the syndicate was a devastating blow.

Reed was arrested and brought to justice, but the damage had been done. The department was left reeling, and the trust that had once bound them together was shattered.

Despite the setbacks, Jack, Lisa, and Viktor pressed on. They knew the fight against the syndicate was far from over, but they were more determined than ever to see it through.

As they continued their work, Viktor's internal conflict remained. He struggled with the weight of his past actions and the desire for redemption. But he knew that as long as he continued to fight against the syndicate, he had a chance to make things right.

The bond between Jack, Lisa, and Viktor grew stronger, forged in the crucible of battle and betrayal. They had faced insurmountable odds and emerged stronger, their resolve unwavering.

As the sun set over Bay City, casting a golden glow over the skyline, Jack felt a renewed sense of purpose. The fight against the syndicate was far from over, but he knew they had the strength and determination to see it through.

The future was uncertain, and the challenges ahead were daunting. But with Lisa and Viktor by his side, Jack knew they could face whatever came their way. The fight for Bay City had only just begun, and they were prepared to see it through to the end.

With each step they took, they moved closer to reclaiming their city from the grip of the syndicate. The battle was far from over, but they were ready for whatever lay ahead. The shadows of betrayal and corruption loomed large, but they knew that together, they could overcome any obstacle.

The fight for Bay City was their mission, their purpose, and they would not rest until justice was served. As the night settled over the city, Jack, Lisa, and Viktor stood ready, prepared to face whatever challenges lay ahead. The future was uncertain, but their resolve was unbreakable. The battle for Bay City had only just begun, and they were prepared to see it through to the end.

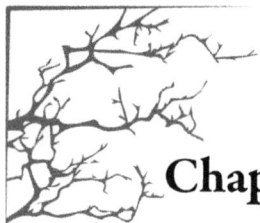

Chapter 8: Cracking the Code

Detective Jack Thompson stared at the cryptic message they had retrieved from the first crime scene. The piece of paper with its seemingly random letters and numbers had been taunting them for weeks. Despite their efforts, the code had remained an enigma, a puzzle that defied all their attempts at resolution. But Jack was not one to give up easily, especially when he knew the key to dismantling the syndicate might lie within those incomprehensible symbols.

Jack sat at his cluttered desk, his mind racing as he examined the coded message once again. His partner, Detective Lisa Ramirez, sat across from him, her expression mirroring his frustration and determination. They had tried everything: frequency analysis, substitution ciphers, even reaching out to cryptographic experts, but the message remained stubbornly opaque.

"I can't shake the feeling that we're missing something obvious," Jack said, his voice tinged with frustration.

Lisa nodded, her brow furrowed in concentration. "Agreed. Maybe we're looking at it the wrong way. We need to think like the syndicate, get inside their heads."

Jack sighed, running a hand through his hair. "Easier said than done. These guys are smart, and they're using a code we haven't seen before."

Just then, Sarah Miller walked into the office, her expression determined. She had been working tirelessly to help them bring down the syndicate, and her knowledge of their operations had been invaluable.

"Any luck with the code?" she asked, taking a seat beside Lisa.

Jack shook his head. "Not yet. We're running out of ideas."

Sarah leaned forward, studying the message. "Let me take a look. Maybe a fresh perspective will help."

For the next few hours, the three of them worked together, trying to crack the code. They went over every possibility, every angle, but the message remained elusive. Frustration mounted, but they refused to give up.

As the night wore on, Lisa suddenly had an epiphany. "Wait a minute," she said, her eyes lighting up. "What if the code isn't just letters and numbers? What if it's a combination of both?"

Jack and Sarah looked at her, intrigued. "Go on," Jack said.

Lisa grabbed a piece of paper and began writing down the letters and numbers from the message. "What if each letter corresponds to a number, and each number corresponds to a letter? It's a substitution cipher, but with a twist."

They watched as Lisa worked, her pen moving quickly across the paper. She wrote out the alphabet and assigned each letter a number, then did the same for the numbers in the message. After a few minutes, she looked up, her eyes wide with excitement.

"I think I've got it," she said, holding up the paper. "Look."

Jack and Sarah leaned in, their eyes scanning the decrypted message. It read:

"Warehouse 13. Midnight."

Jack's heart raced. They had finally cracked the code, and it was pointing them to an abandoned warehouse – a place that could potentially be a major hub for the syndicate's operations.

"This is it," Jack said, his voice filled with determination. "Warehouse 13. We need to move fast."

They quickly gathered their gear and headed out, the adrenaline pumping through their veins. The warehouse was located in a desolate part of the city, an area known for its abandoned buildings and criminal activity. It was the perfect place for the syndicate to operate under the radar.

As they approached the warehouse, Jack and Lisa moved cautiously, their senses on high alert. The building loomed ahead of them, its windows shattered and its walls covered in graffiti. It was eerily silent, the only sound the crunch of gravel under their boots.

"Stay sharp," Jack whispered. "This could be a trap."

They circled the building, looking for a way in. They found a side door that had been left ajar, and Jack signaled for Lisa and Sarah to follow him. They entered the warehouse, their flashlights cutting through the darkness.

The interior was a labyrinth of old machinery, rusted catwalks, and stacks of crates. The air was thick with dust, and the faint smell of decay lingered. They moved quietly, their footsteps echoing in the vast, empty space.

Suddenly, a noise ahead caught Jack's attention. He raised his hand, signaling for the others to stop. They listened intently, straining to hear over the pounding of their hearts.

"Did you hear that?" Lisa whispered.

Jack nodded, his grip tightening on his weapon. "Someone's here."

They moved forward cautiously, their flashlights illuminating the path ahead. As they rounded a corner, they saw a group of men huddled around a table, examining what appeared to be blueprints.

"Drop your weapons!" Jack shouted, his voice echoing through the warehouse.

The men turned, their faces registering shock and anger. Without warning, they drew their guns and opened fire. Jack, Lisa, and Sarah dove for cover, the bullets whizzing past them and ricocheting off the walls.

The firefight was intense, the air filled with the deafening sound of gunfire and the acrid smell of gunpowder. Jack and Lisa returned fire, their training and experience guiding their every move. Sarah moved to flank the attackers, her movements quick and precise.

As the battle raged on, Jack noticed something strange. The men they were fighting seemed unusually well-prepared, as if they had been expecting them. The realization hit him like a punch to the gut.

"It's a trap!" he shouted to Lisa and Sarah. "We need to get out of here!"

They began to retreat, moving back toward the entrance. But the men pursued them relentlessly, their gunfire pinning them down. Jack knew they were in a dire situation, but he refused to give up.

"Follow me!" he shouted, leading them through a maze of crates and machinery.

They moved quickly, their hearts pounding as they navigated the labyrinthine interior of the warehouse. The gunfire continued, the bullets tearing through the air around them. Jack could feel the adrenaline coursing through his veins, his mind focused on survival.

As they neared the entrance, a deafening explosion rocked the building. Jack was thrown to the ground, his ears ringing and his vision blurred. He struggled to his feet, his mind racing.

"Lisa! Sarah!" he shouted, his voice barely audible over the ringing in his ears.

He saw Lisa nearby, struggling to stand. He rushed to her side, helping her to her feet. "Are you okay?" he asked, his voice filled with concern.

Lisa nodded, though she looked shaken. "Yeah, I'm fine. Where's Sarah?"

They looked around, their eyes scanning the chaos. They spotted Sarah a few yards away, pinned under a pile of debris. Jack and Lisa rushed to her side, their hearts pounding with fear.

"Sarah, hold on!" Jack shouted, his voice filled with determination.

They worked quickly, lifting the debris and freeing Sarah. She was conscious but clearly in pain, her leg twisted at an unnatural angle.

"We need to get out of here," Jack said, his voice urgent. "Can you walk?"

Sarah gritted her teeth and nodded. "I'll manage."

With Lisa's help, Jack lifted Sarah to her feet. They moved as quickly as they could, their eyes constantly scanning for danger. The warehouse was collapsing around them, the fire from the explosion spreading rapidly.

As they neared the exit, they encountered more of the syndicate's men. The firefight resumed, but this time Jack and Lisa were determined to fight their way out. They moved with precision and focus, their every action guided by their training and instincts.

Finally, they reached the door and burst out into the night. The cool air hit them like a refreshing wave, and they breathed a collective sigh of relief. But they knew they weren't out of danger yet.

"Get to the car!" Jack shouted, his voice filled with urgency.

They ran to their vehicle, helping Sarah into the back seat. Jack jumped into the driver's seat, and Lisa took the passenger seat. As they sped away from the burning warehouse, Jack glanced in the rearview mirror, his mind racing.

"We need to get Sarah to a hospital," he said, his voice filled with concern.

Lisa nodded. "Agreed. And we need to regroup. This isn't over."

They drove to the nearest hospital, where they managed to get Sarah admitted without drawing too much attention. As they waited in the emergency room, the weight of the night's events settled heavily on their shoulders.

"This was a setup," Jack said, his voice filled with frustration. "They knew we were coming."

Lisa nodded, her expression grim. "Someone tipped them off. We need to find out who and why."

After ensuring Sarah was in good hands, Jack and Lisa returned to the precinct. They gathered their team and reviewed the events of the night, trying to piece together what had gone wrong.

"We need to figure out how they knew we were coming," Jack said, his voice filled with determination. "And we need to be more careful. We can't afford any more mistakes."

They began to investigate, questioning everyone who had access to the coded message and their plans. The atmosphere within the department was tense, with everyone on edge and suspicious of each other.

As the days passed, they uncovered more evidence of the syndicate's reach and influence. It became clear that they had been infiltrated at the highest levels, and the betrayal cut deep.

Jack and Lisa knew they needed to take a different approach. They began to work more covertly, keeping their plans tightly guarded and only sharing information on a need-to-know basis. The stakes were higher than ever, and they couldn't afford any more leaks.

One evening, as they worked late in the precinct, Jack received a call from an anonymous source. The voice on the other end was distorted, but the message was clear.

"I know who the mole is," the voice said. "Meet me at the old factory on Fifth Street. Midnight. Come alone."

Jack's heart raced as he hung up the phone. He knew it was a risk, but he also knew they needed answers.

He shared the information with Lisa, and they devised a plan. Jack would go to the meeting, but he wouldn't be alone. Lisa and a backup team would be nearby, ready to move in if things went south.

As midnight approached, Jack made his way to the old factory. The building was dark and foreboding, its windows boarded up and its walls covered in graffiti. He entered cautiously, his senses on high alert.

"Hello?" he called out, his voice echoing through the empty space.

A figure emerged from the shadows, their face obscured by a hood. "Detective Thompson," the figure said, their voice still distorted. "I have information for you."

Jack's hand tightened on his weapon. "Who are you?"

"That doesn't matter," the figure replied. "What matters is that I know who the mole is."

Jack listened intently as the figure revealed the identity of the mole – Officer James Collins. The same officer who had previously been under suspicion but had managed to evade detection.

"Collins has been feeding the syndicate information for months," the figure said. "He's the reason your operations have been compromised."

Jack's mind raced. He knew they needed to act quickly to apprehend Collins and prevent any further leaks.

"Why are you telling me this?" Jack asked, his voice filled with suspicion.

"Because I want to see the syndicate brought down," the figure replied. "And I believe you can do it."

Before Jack could ask any more questions, the figure disappeared into the shadows. He knew he had no time to waste. He contacted Lisa and the backup team, informing them of the new information.

They moved quickly, apprehending Collins at his home and bringing him in for questioning. The betrayal was a bitter pill to swallow, but they knew they needed to stay focused.

Under interrogation, Collins eventually broke down and confessed. He revealed the extent of his involvement with the syndicate and provided valuable information about their operations.

With Collins in custody, Jack and Lisa felt a renewed sense of determination. They knew they had a long road ahead, but they were more determined than ever to bring down the syndicate.

As they continued their investigation, they uncovered more evidence of the syndicate's operations and began to dismantle their networks piece by piece. The battle was far from over, but they were making progress.

One evening, as they worked late in the precinct, Jack received another call from the anonymous source.

"You've made progress," the voice said. "But there's still more to do. The syndicate is planning something big, and you need to be ready."

"What are they planning?" Jack asked, his voice filled with urgency.

"All in due time," the voice replied. "Just be prepared."

With that ominous warning hanging over them, Jack and Lisa knew they needed to stay vigilant. The syndicate was a formidable foe, but they were determined to see it through to the end.

As the sun set over Bay City, casting a golden glow over the skyline, Jack felt a renewed sense of purpose. The fight against the syndicate was far from over, but he knew they had the strength and determination to see it through.

The future was uncertain, and the challenges ahead were daunting. But with Lisa and Sarah by his side, Jack knew they could face whatever came their way. The fight for Bay City had only just begun, and they were prepared to see it through to the end.

With each step they took, they moved closer to reclaiming their city from the grip of the syndicate. The battle was far from over, but they were ready for whatever lay ahead. The shadows of betrayal and corruption loomed large, but they knew that together, they could overcome any obstacle.

The fight for Bay City was their mission, their purpose, and they would not rest until justice was served. As the night settled over the city, Jack, Lisa, and Sarah stood ready, prepared to face whatever challenges lay ahead. The future was uncertain, but their resolve was unbreakable. The battle for Bay City had only just begun, and they were prepared to see it through to the end.

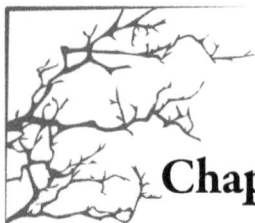

Chapter 9: Allies and Enemies

Detective Jack Thompson stood in the war room of the Bay City Police Department, staring at the cluttered whiteboard that outlined their battle against the syndicate. The room was buzzing with activity as officers moved about, organizing files and strategizing for their next moves. Jack knew that to truly bring down the syndicate, they needed more than just the resources of their own department. They needed allies, and they needed them now.

Jack turned to his partner, Detective Lisa Ramirez, who was deep in conversation with Sarah Miller. Sarah's infiltration of the syndicate had given them invaluable intel, but the stakes were getting higher with each passing day.

"We need to expand our reach," Jack said, interrupting their discussion. "We can't do this alone. It's time to bring in other agencies."

Lisa nodded, her expression serious. "I agree. We've been running ourselves ragged trying to stay ahead of the syndicate. If we're going to take them down, we need all the help we can get."

Sarah added, "We also need to be careful about who we trust. The syndicate's influence runs deep, and we can't afford any more leaks."

Jack nodded. "Let's start with the DEA and the FBI. They've both got a vested interest in dismantling organized crime, and they have the resources we need."

The next day, Jack and Lisa set up meetings with representatives from the DEA and the FBI. The DEA had been tracking the syndicate's drug operations for years, while the FBI had been investigating their involvement in various federal crimes. The meetings were tense but productive, with both agencies agreeing to share information and coordinate efforts.

Special Agent Rachel Morgan from the FBI was a seasoned investigator with a no-nonsense attitude. She had a reputation for getting results, and Jack knew she would be a valuable ally. Meanwhile, Agent Tom Bennett from the

DEA brought a wealth of knowledge about the syndicate's drug trafficking routes and distribution networks.

As they sat around the conference table, poring over maps and intelligence reports, Jack felt a renewed sense of determination. They were building a coalition, one that could finally bring the syndicate to its knees.

"Thank you all for being here," Jack said, addressing the group. "The syndicate is a threat to all of us, and it's going to take a united effort to bring them down. We've made progress, but we need to stay one step ahead."

Agent Morgan nodded. "We've been tracking their financial transactions and have identified several key players. With your intel, we can start building a more complete picture of their operations."

Agent Bennett added, "We've also got leads on their drug supply chain. If we can cut off their supply, we can cripple their operations."

Lisa spoke up. "We've also got a potential new ally. There's a rival gang leader who's reached out to us. He claims to have inside information on the syndicate and wants to make a deal."

Jack's eyebrows raised in surprise. "A rival gang leader? That's risky. What's his angle?"

"He's looking to take down the syndicate for his own reasons," Lisa explained. "But he's willing to share what he knows in exchange for protection and a reduced sentence for his people."

Agent Morgan looked skeptical. "Can we trust him?"

Lisa shrugged. "We don't have much choice. If his information checks out, it could be a game-changer. But we'll need to approach this carefully."

Jack nodded. "Let's set up a meeting. We'll need to vet him thoroughly and ensure he's not leading us into a trap."

The meeting with the rival gang leader, Marcus "Mack" Reynolds, was arranged in a neutral location – an abandoned warehouse on the outskirts of the city. The choice of venue was deliberate, a place where both sides could feel secure and where an ambush would be less likely.

Jack, Lisa, and Sarah arrived early, accompanied by a contingent of heavily armed officers. They set up a secure perimeter and prepared for the arrival of Mack and his men. The tension was palpable, and everyone was on edge.

Mack arrived shortly after, flanked by his lieutenants. He was a tall, imposing figure with a scar running down the side of his face – a souvenir from a past encounter with the syndicate. Despite his rough appearance, his eyes were sharp and intelligent.

"Detective Thompson, Detective Ramirez," Mack said, nodding in acknowledgment. "Thank you for agreeing to meet."

Jack stepped forward, extending a hand. "Marcus Reynolds, I presume. Let's get straight to the point. What do you have for us?"

Mack shook Jack's hand, his grip firm. "I have information that can help you take down the syndicate's leadership. They've been a thorn in my side for too long, and it's time they were removed."

Lisa crossed her arms, her gaze piercing. "Why now? Why come to us?"

Mack sighed, his expression hardening. "Because they've crossed a line. They've started targeting my people, and I won't stand for it. I'm willing to make a deal, but I need assurances."

Jack nodded. "We're willing to listen. But understand this – we don't make deals lightly. Your information needs to be solid."

Mack gestured to one of his lieutenants, who stepped forward with a folder. "Here's a start. Financial records, shipment schedules, names of key players. This is just the tip of the iceberg."

Jack took the folder, flipping through its contents. It was a treasure trove of information, enough to make a significant impact on their investigation.

"This is good," Jack said, his voice measured. "But we'll need more. And we'll need to verify everything."

Mack nodded. "I understand. I'll give you what you need, but I want protection for my people. We can't operate in this city with the syndicate breathing down our necks."

Lisa leaned in, her voice firm. "You help us take down the syndicate, and we'll make sure you and your people are protected. But cross us, and there will be consequences."

Mack met her gaze, unflinching. "Understood. Let's get to work."

The uneasy alliance was forged, and over the next few weeks, Mack provided a steady stream of information. His intel was invaluable, shedding light on the syndicate's inner workings and giving Jack and Lisa the edge they needed.

Despite the progress, the atmosphere remained tense. The syndicate was aware that their operations were being disrupted, and their retaliation was swift and brutal. Several officers were targeted, and the pressure on Jack and Lisa intensified.

One evening, as they reviewed the latest intelligence, Sarah approached with a look of concern. "We've intercepted a message from the syndicate. They're planning a major operation, something big. We need to act fast."

Jack's heart raced. "What do we know?"

Sarah handed him a decoded message. "It's going down tomorrow night. They're planning to hit a major shipment at the docks. If we can intercept it, we can deal a significant blow."

Lisa frowned. "But it's a trap, isn't it? They'll be expecting us."

Jack nodded. "Most likely. But we can't afford to pass up this opportunity. We'll need to be smart about this."

They spent the next few hours planning the operation, coordinating with their new allies from the DEA and the FBI. The goal was to intercept the shipment, capture key members of the syndicate, and gather as much evidence as possible.

As night fell, they moved out, their hearts pounding with anticipation. The docks were a sprawling complex, a maze of shipping containers and warehouses. It was the perfect place for an ambush, and they knew they had to be prepared for anything.

Jack, Lisa, and Sarah led the main assault team, while Agents Morgan and Bennett coordinated from a mobile command center. Mack and his men provided additional support, their presence a reminder of the uneasy truce they had forged.

As they approached the designated area, Jack's senses were on high alert. The air was thick with tension, and every shadow seemed to conceal a potential threat.

"Stay sharp," he whispered to his team. "We move in on my signal."

They crept forward, their movements silent and coordinated. As they neared the shipping containers, they saw the syndicate members unloading crates from a cargo ship. The men were heavily armed, and their expressions were tense.

"Now," Jack signaled.

They moved in quickly, catching the syndicate members off guard. A firefight erupted, the air filled with the sound of gunfire and the acrid smell of gunpowder. Jack and Lisa fought with precision and determination, their every move calculated.

Sarah provided cover fire, her sharpshooting skills proving invaluable. Mack and his men moved in from the flanks, their presence turning the tide of the battle.

Despite the chaos, Jack's focus remained unwavering. He spotted a familiar figure – Victor Morales, one of the syndicate's top lieutenants. Jack knew that capturing Victor could be a game-changer.

"Lisa, cover me!" Jack shouted, charging towards Victor.

Lisa provided cover fire as Jack tackled Victor to the ground, their struggle intense. Victor fought back fiercely, but Jack's determination gave him the edge.

"Give it up, Victor," Jack growled. "It's over."

Victor sneered, his eyes filled with hatred. "You think you can stop us? We're everywhere."

Jack tightened his grip, his voice cold. "We'll see about that."

With Victor in custody and the syndicate members either captured or neutralized, the operation was a success. They gathered evidence from the crates, uncovering a cache of weapons, drugs, and financial records that would prove invaluable in their ongoing investigation.

As they regrouped at the mobile command center, the sense of victory was tempered by the knowledge that the battle was far from over. The syndicate was a formidable foe, and they knew that their retaliation would be swift and brutal.

Agent Morgan approached, her expression serious. "Good work tonight. But we need to stay on our guard. The syndicate won't take this lying down."

Agent Bennett added, "We've made significant progress, but we need to keep the pressure on. The more we disrupt their operations, the more desperate they'll become."

Jack nodded, his resolve unwavering. "Agreed. We're in this for the long haul. We can't afford to let up now."

Over the next few weeks, the coalition of law enforcement agencies continued their efforts to dismantle the syndicate. They conducted raids, intercepted shipments, and gathered intelligence, all while keeping a close watch on their new allies.

The uneasy alliance with Mack and his gang proved to be both a blessing and a curse. While Mack's information was invaluable, the tension between the two groups remained high. Trust was a fragile commodity, and both sides knew that betrayal was always a possibility.

One evening, as Jack and Lisa reviewed the latest intelligence reports, they received an unexpected visitor. Mack entered their office, his expression serious.

"We need to talk," Mack said, taking a seat.

Jack looked at him, his eyes wary. "What's on your mind?"

Mack sighed. "The syndicate is planning something big. Bigger than anything we've seen so far. They're bringing in a new player, someone with serious firepower."

Lisa frowned. "Who?"

Mack's expression darkened. "Ivan Romanov. He's a major arms dealer with connections all over Eastern Europe. If he's involved, it means the syndicate is gearing up for a full-scale war."

Jack's heart sank. The introduction of Romanov into the equation was a game-changer, and it meant that the stakes were higher than ever.

"We need to take him down," Jack said, his voice filled with determination. "Before he can establish a foothold."

Mack nodded. "Agreed. But it won't be easy. Romanov is heavily protected, and his operations are well-guarded. We'll need to be smart about this."

Lisa leaned forward, her eyes focused. "Do you have any intel on his operations? Anything we can use?"

Mack handed her a folder. "This is everything I've got. Locations, names, shipment schedules. It's not complete, but it's a start."

Jack took the folder, his mind racing. "This is good. We'll need to coordinate with the DEA and the FBI. If we can hit Romanov hard, we can disrupt the syndicate's plans."

The next few days were a whirlwind of activity as they prepared for the operation. They coordinated with their allies, sharing intelligence and strategizing their approach. The goal was to intercept a major shipment of arms that Romanov was bringing into the city, a shipment that could tip the balance of power in the syndicate's favor.

As night fell, they moved out, their hearts pounding with anticipation. The location was a sprawling warehouse complex near the docks, a place that was both heavily guarded and strategically important.

Jack, Lisa, and Sarah led the main assault team, while Agents Morgan and Bennett coordinated from a mobile command center. Mack and his men provided additional support, their presence a reminder of the uneasy truce they had forged.

As they approached the complex, Jack's senses were on high alert. The air was thick with tension, and every shadow seemed to conceal a potential threat.

"Stay sharp," he whispered to his team. "We move in on my signal."

They crept forward, their movements silent and coordinated. As they neared the entrance, they saw the syndicate members unloading crates from a cargo truck. The men were heavily armed, and their expressions were tense.

"Now," Jack signaled.

They moved in quickly, catching the syndicate members off guard. A firefight erupted, the air filled with the sound of gunfire and the acrid smell of gunpowder. Jack and Lisa fought with precision and determination, their every move calculated.

Sarah provided cover fire, her sharpshooting skills proving invaluable. Mack and his men moved in from the flanks, their presence turning the tide of the battle.

Despite the chaos, Jack's focus remained unwavering. He spotted a familiar figure – Ivan Romanov, orchestrating the operation from a makeshift command center. Jack knew that capturing Romanov could be a game-changer.

"Lisa, cover me!" Jack shouted, charging towards Romanov.

Lisa provided cover fire as Jack tackled Romanov to the ground, their struggle intense. Romanov fought back fiercely, but Jack's determination gave him the edge.

"Give it up, Romanov," Jack growled. "It's over."

Romanov sneered, his eyes filled with hatred. "You think you can stop us? We're everywhere."

Jack tightened his grip, his voice cold. "We'll see about that."

With Romanov in custody and the syndicate members either captured or neutralized, the operation was a success. They gathered evidence from the crates, uncovering a cache of weapons and financial records that would prove invaluable in their ongoing investigation.

As they regrouped at the mobile command center, the sense of victory was tempered by the knowledge that the battle was far from over. The syndicate was a formidable foe, and they knew that their retaliation would be swift and brutal.

Agent Morgan approached, her expression serious. "Good work tonight. But we need to stay on our guard. The syndicate won't take this lying down."

Agent Bennett added, "We've made significant progress, but we need to keep the pressure on. The more we disrupt their operations, the more desperate they'll become."

Jack nodded, his resolve unwavering. "Agreed. We're in this for the long haul. We can't afford to let up now."

Over the next few weeks, the coalition of law enforcement agencies continued their efforts to dismantle the syndicate. They conducted raids, intercepted shipments, and gathered intelligence, all while keeping a close watch on their new allies.

The uneasy alliance with Mack and his gang proved to be both a blessing and a curse. While Mack's information was invaluable, the tension between the two groups remained high. Trust was a fragile commodity, and both sides knew that betrayal was always a possibility.

One evening, as Jack and Lisa reviewed the latest intelligence reports, they received an unexpected visitor. Mack entered their office, his expression serious.

"We need to talk," Mack said, taking a seat.

Jack looked at him, his eyes wary. "What's on your mind?"

Mack sighed. "The syndicate is planning something big. Bigger than anything we've seen so far. They're bringing in a new player, someone with serious firepower."

Lisa frowned. "Who?"

Mack's expression darkened. "Ivan Romanov. He's a major arms dealer with connections all over Eastern Europe. If he's involved, it means the syndicate is gearing up for a full-scale war."

Jack's heart sank. The introduction of Romanov into the equation was a game-changer, and it meant that the stakes were higher than ever.

"We need to take him down," Jack said, his voice filled with determination. "Before he can establish a foothold."

Mack nodded. "Agreed. But it won't be easy. Romanov is heavily protected, and his operations are well-guarded. We'll need to be smart about this."

Lisa leaned forward, her eyes focused. "Do you have any intel on his operations? Anything we can use?"

Mack handed her a folder. "This is everything I've got. Locations, names, shipment schedules. It's not complete, but it's a start."

Jack took the folder, his mind racing. "This is good. We'll need to coordinate with the DEA and the FBI. If we can hit Romanov hard, we can disrupt the syndicate's plans."

The next few days were a whirlwind of activity as they prepared for the operation. They coordinated with their allies, sharing intelligence and strategizing their approach. The goal was to intercept a major shipment of arms that Romanov was bringing into the city, a shipment that could tip the balance of power in the syndicate's favor.

As night fell, they moved out, their hearts pounding with anticipation. The location was a sprawling warehouse complex near the docks, a place that was both heavily guarded and strategically important.

Jack, Lisa, and Sarah led the main assault team, while Agents Morgan and Bennett coordinated from a mobile command center. Mack and his men provided additional support, their presence a reminder of the uneasy truce they had forged.

As they approached the complex, Jack's senses were on high alert. The air was thick with tension, and every shadow seemed to conceal a potential threat.

"Stay sharp," he whispered to his team. "We move in on my signal."

They crept forward, their movements silent and coordinated. As they neared the entrance, they saw the syndicate members unloading crates from a cargo truck. The men were heavily armed, and their expressions were tense.

"Now," Jack signaled.

They moved in quickly, catching the syndicate members off guard. A firefight erupted, the air filled with the sound of gunfire and the acrid smell of gunpowder. Jack and Lisa fought with precision and determination, their every move calculated.

Sarah provided cover fire, her sharpshooting skills proving invaluable. Mack and his men moved in from the flanks, their presence turning the tide of the battle.

Despite the chaos, Jack's focus remained unwavering. He spotted a familiar figure – Ivan Romanov, orchestrating the operation from a makeshift command center. Jack knew that capturing Romanov could be a game-changer.

"Lisa, cover me!" Jack shouted, charging towards Romanov.

Lisa provided cover fire as Jack tackled Romanov to the ground, their struggle intense. Romanov fought back fiercely, but Jack's determination gave him the edge.

"Give it up, Romanov," Jack growled. "It's over."

Romanov sneered, his eyes filled with hatred. "You think you can stop us? We're everywhere."

Jack tightened his grip, his voice cold. "We'll see about that."

With Romanov in custody and the syndicate members either captured or neutralized, the operation was a success. They gathered evidence from the crates, uncovering a cache of weapons and financial records that would prove invaluable in their ongoing investigation.

As they regrouped at the mobile command center, the sense of victory was tempered by the knowledge that the battle was far from over. The syndicate was a formidable foe, and they knew that their retaliation would be swift and brutal.

Agent Morgan approached, her expression serious. "Good work tonight. But we need to stay on our guard. The syndicate won't take this lying down."

Agent Bennett added, "We've made significant progress, but we need to keep the pressure on. The more we disrupt their operations, the more desperate they'll become."

Jack nodded, his resolve unwavering. "Agreed. We're in this for the long haul. We can't afford to let up now."

Over the next few weeks, the coalition of law enforcement agencies continued their efforts to dismantle the syndicate. They conducted raids, intercepted shipments, and gathered intelligence, all while keeping a close watch on their new allies.

The uneasy alliance with Mack and his gang proved to be both a blessing and a curse. While Mack's information was invaluable, the tension between the two groups remained high. Trust was a fragile commodity, and both sides knew that betrayal was always a possibility.

As they continued their work, Jack felt a renewed sense of purpose. The fight against the syndicate was far from over, but he knew they had the strength and determination to see it through.

The future was uncertain, and the challenges ahead were daunting. But with Lisa and Sarah by his side, Jack knew they could face whatever came their way. The fight for Bay City had only just begun, and they were prepared to see it through to the end.

With each step they took, they moved closer to reclaiming their city from the grip of the syndicate. The battle was far from over, but they were ready for whatever lay ahead. The shadows of betrayal and corruption loomed large, but they knew that together, they could overcome any obstacle.

The fight for Bay City was their mission, their purpose, and they would not rest until justice was served. As the night settled over the city, Jack, Lisa, and Sarah stood ready, prepared to face whatever challenges lay ahead. The future was uncertain, but their resolve was unbreakable. The battle for Bay City had only just begun, and they were prepared to see it through to the end.

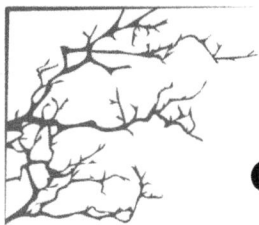

Chapter 10: The Wolf Unmasked

The room was filled with the quiet hum of computers and the rustle of papers. Detectives Jack Thompson and Lisa Ramirez sat in their usual spots, surrounded by a mountain of files and evidence. It had been months since they first began their relentless pursuit of the syndicate, and each day brought them closer to their ultimate goal: unmasking and capturing "The Wolf," the enigmatic leader of the crime organization that had plagued Bay City.

Across the room, Sarah Miller was deeply engrossed in her own work. She had been the linchpin in their operation, providing invaluable insights and intelligence from her time undercover. Now, she was on the verge of a breakthrough.

"Jack, Lisa, come here," Sarah called, her voice tinged with urgency.

Jack and Lisa quickly joined her, their expressions a mix of curiosity and anticipation.

"I think I've got something," Sarah said, her eyes scanning the screen in front of her. "I've been cross-referencing all the data we've gathered, and I believe I've finally identified 'The Wolf.'"

Jack's heart skipped a beat. "Who is he?"

Sarah took a deep breath. "His real name is Viktor Ivanov, but he's been using the alias 'The Wolf' to maintain his anonymity. He's a former Russian intelligence officer who turned to organized crime after the collapse of the Soviet Union. He's been operating under the radar for years, building his empire and avoiding detection."

Lisa's eyes widened. "Viktor Ivanov... that explains a lot. His military training, his strategic mind. No wonder he's been so elusive."

Sarah nodded. "I've also uncovered his plans. He's been orchestrating a series of high-profile assassinations and kidnappings, targeting key figures in law enforcement and politics. His goal is to destabilize the city and take control."

Jack's mind raced. "We need to act fast. If we can take down Ivanov, we can dismantle the syndicate and prevent any more bloodshed."

Lisa agreed. "But we need to be careful. He's dangerous and well-protected. We'll need to plan this operation meticulously."

They spent the next few hours devising a plan to raid the syndicate's headquarters, a heavily fortified compound on the outskirts of the city. The compound was equipped with state-of-the-art security systems and guarded by Ivanov's most loyal men. It was a daunting task, but Jack, Lisa, and Sarah were determined to see it through.

They coordinated with their allies from the DEA and the FBI, securing additional resources and manpower for the raid. The operation was set to take place under the cover of darkness, maximizing their chances of catching Ivanov off guard.

As night fell, the team assembled at a staging area near the compound. The air was thick with tension, and the gravity of the mission weighed heavily on everyone's shoulders. Jack addressed the assembled officers, his voice steady and authoritative.

"Listen up, everyone. This is it. We've been working towards this moment for months. Viktor Ivanov, aka 'The Wolf,' is our primary target. We need to move quickly and efficiently. Our goal is to capture him and gather as much evidence as possible. Stay sharp, stay focused, and watch each other's backs. Let's bring him down."

The team moved out, their movements silent and coordinated. As they approached the compound, they encountered the first line of security – a series of motion sensors and surveillance cameras. Using the intel provided by Sarah, they disabled the systems and advanced undetected.

They reached the perimeter of the compound, where they encountered the first guards. The guards were heavily armed and alert, but Jack and his team were prepared. They moved in swiftly, taking down the guards with a combination of stealth and precision.

As they breached the compound, chaos erupted. The sound of gunfire echoed through the halls, and the air was filled with the acrid smell of gunpowder. Jack and Lisa led the assault, their movements fluid and coordinated. Sarah provided cover fire, her sharpshooting skills proving invaluable.

Despite the chaos, Jack's focus remained unwavering. He knew that capturing Ivanov was the key to dismantling the syndicate. They fought their way through the compound, clearing room after room, until they reached a heavily reinforced door – Ivanov's command center.

"Lisa, cover me," Jack ordered, preparing to breach the door.

Lisa nodded, her weapon at the ready. "On it."

They burst into the room, guns drawn, ready for anything. Ivanov was there, surrounded by his top lieutenants. He looked up, a cold, calculating smile playing on his lips.

"Detective Thompson," Ivanov said, his voice smooth and unflappable. "I must admit, I'm impressed. You've been a worthy adversary."

Jack's eyes narrowed. "It's over, Ivanov. Surrender now, and no one else has to get hurt."

Ivanov's smile widened. "You think you can stop me? You have no idea what you're up against."

Before Jack could react, Ivanov activated a hidden switch, and the room filled with a blinding flash of light. Jack and Lisa were thrown to the ground, their senses overwhelmed by the sudden explosion.

When the dust settled, Ivanov and his lieutenants were gone, leaving behind a scene of destruction. Jack struggled to his feet, his ears ringing and his vision blurred.

"Lisa, are you okay?" he called out, his voice strained.

Lisa groaned, pushing herself up from the debris. "Yeah, I'm fine. But Ivanov got away."

Jack's frustration boiled over. "Damn it! We were so close."

Sarah joined them, her expression grim. "We need to regroup. Ivanov's still out there, and he won't stop until he's achieved his goals."

They quickly secured the compound, apprehending the remaining syndicate members and gathering as much evidence as possible. Despite Ivanov's escape, the operation was a success. They had dealt a significant blow to the syndicate's operations and uncovered crucial information about their plans.

Back at the precinct, Jack, Lisa, and Sarah reviewed the evidence they had collected. Among the documents were detailed plans for the assassinations and kidnappings Ivanov had been orchestrating. They also found a list of names – key figures in law enforcement and politics who were targeted by the syndicate.

"We need to warn these people," Lisa said, her voice urgent. "They're in grave danger."

Jack nodded. "Agreed. We also need to continue our pursuit of Ivanov. He's not going to stop, and neither can we."

Over the next few days, they worked tirelessly to protect the individuals on Ivanov's hit list, coordinating with local and federal authorities to provide security and thwart any assassination attempts. Their efforts paid off, and several high-profile targets were saved from imminent danger.

Meanwhile, they continued their pursuit of Ivanov, following every lead and scrutinizing every piece of evidence. It was a grueling process, but they were determined to see it through.

One evening, as they pored over the latest intelligence reports, Sarah made a startling discovery. Hidden within the documents they had recovered from the compound was a coded message – a message that hinted at a larger conspiracy.

"Jack, Lisa, look at this," Sarah said, pointing to the screen. "I think this message is from Ivanov. It mentions something called 'Operation Phoenix.'"

Jack's eyes narrowed. "Operation Phoenix? What is that?"

Sarah began decoding the message, her fingers flying across the keyboard. "From what I can gather, it's a plan to destabilize the city by targeting critical infrastructure – power plants, water supply, transportation networks. Ivanov's trying to create chaos on a massive scale."

Lisa's expression hardened. "We need to stop this. If Ivanov succeeds, it could be catastrophic."

Jack agreed. "We need to find out where and when this is going to happen. We can't let Ivanov execute his plan."

They spent the next few hours deciphering the message and analyzing the data. It was a race against time, but their efforts paid off. They discovered that Ivanov was planning to launch Operation Phoenix in three days, using a series of coordinated attacks to bring the city to its knees.

Armed with this knowledge, they mobilized their forces, coordinating with local and federal agencies to prevent the attacks. The city was placed on high alert, and security was heightened at all critical infrastructure sites.

As the day of the planned attacks approached, the tension was palpable. Jack, Lisa, and Sarah worked around the clock, monitoring the situation and coordinating their response.

Finally, the day arrived. The city was on edge, but they were ready. Jack and Lisa led the main response team, while Sarah provided crucial intelligence from their command center.

As they monitored the situation, they received word that Ivanov had been spotted near one of the power plants. Jack's heart raced. This was their chance to capture him and put an end to his plans.

"Let's move," Jack ordered, leading his team to the location.

They arrived at the power plant, where they found Ivanov and his men preparing to launch their attack. The air was thick with tension as they approached, their weapons at the ready.

"Drop your weapons!" Jack shouted, his voice echoing through the facility.

Ivanov turned to face them, a cold smile playing on his lips. "Ah, Detective Thompson. Right on time."

The firefight erupted, the sound of gunfire echoing through the plant. Jack and Lisa fought with precision and determination, their every move calculated. Sarah provided crucial intelligence, guiding them through the chaos.

Despite the intense battle, Ivanov remained a formidable adversary. He moved with the precision of a trained soldier, his every action calculated and deadly.

As the fight raged on, Jack finally managed to corner Ivanov. Their eyes locked, and Jack felt a surge of determination.

"It's over, Ivanov," Jack growled. "You're done."

Ivanov's smile never wavered. "You think you've won, Detective? This is just the beginning."

Before Jack could react, Ivanov activated a hidden detonator, triggering a series of explosions. The facility shook, and Jack was thrown to the ground.

When the dust settled, Ivanov was gone, leaving behind a trail of destruction. Jack struggled to his feet, his mind racing.

"Lisa, are you okay?" he called out.

Lisa groaned, pushing herself up from the debris. "Yeah, I'm fine. But Ivanov escaped."

Jack's frustration boiled over. "Damn it! We were so close."

Sarah's voice crackled over the radio. "Jack, we need to regroup. There's more at stake here than we realized."

Jack and Lisa made their way back to the command center, where they reviewed the latest intelligence. They discovered that Ivanov's escape was part of a larger conspiracy – a network of criminal organizations working together to destabilize the city.

"We're dealing with something much bigger than we thought," Sarah said, her voice filled with determination. "We need to keep digging, keep fighting."

Jack nodded, his resolve unwavering. "Agreed. Ivanov may have escaped, but we won't stop until we've brought him and his entire network to justice."

Over the next few weeks, they continued their pursuit of Ivanov, following every lead and scrutinizing every piece of evidence. The battle was far from over, but they were more determined than ever to see it through.

One evening, as they worked late in the precinct, Jack received an unexpected call. The voice on the other end was familiar – it was the anonymous source who had provided them with crucial information in the past.

"Detective Thompson," the voice said, "I have information about Ivanov's next move. He's planning something big, and you need to be ready."

"What is he planning?" Jack asked, his voice filled with urgency.

"I can't say much, but it's going to happen soon. Be prepared," the voice replied before hanging up.

With the ominous warning hanging over them, Jack, Lisa, and Sarah knew they needed to stay vigilant. The fight against Ivanov and his network was far from over, but they were ready for whatever came their way.

As the sun set over Bay City, casting a golden glow over the skyline, Jack felt a renewed sense of purpose. The battle against Ivanov was a long and arduous one, but he knew they had the strength and determination to see it through.

The future was uncertain, and the challenges ahead were daunting. But with Lisa and Sarah by his side, Jack knew they could face whatever came their way. The fight for Bay City had only just begun, and they were prepared to see it through to the end.

With each step they took, they moved closer to reclaiming their city from the grip of Ivanov and his network. The battle was far from over, but they were ready for whatever lay ahead. The shadows of betrayal and corruption loomed large, but they knew that together, they could overcome any obstacle.

The fight for Bay City was their mission, their purpose, and they would not rest until justice was served. As the night settled over the city, Jack, Lisa, and Sarah stood ready, prepared to face whatever challenges lay ahead. The future was uncertain, but their resolve was unbreakable. The battle for Bay City had only just begun, and they were prepared to see it through to the end.

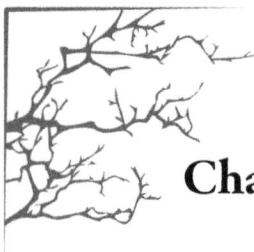

Chapter 11: The Safe House

The tension was palpable as Jack Thompson, Lisa Ramirez, and Sarah Miller sat in the dimly lit room of the safe house. The worn furniture and peeling wallpaper contrasted sharply with the state-of-the-art surveillance equipment they had set up around them. This safe house, a nondescript building in a secluded part of Bay City, had become their refuge as they regrouped and planned their next move against Viktor Ivanov, also known as "The Wolf."

The air was thick with the weight of their recent failures and the looming threat of Ivanov's next move. Jack's jaw was clenched, his mind racing with thoughts of how close they had come to capturing Ivanov, only to have him slip through their fingers once again. Lisa and Sarah were equally tense, their eyes betraying the exhaustion and frustration that had been building up over the past few weeks.

"We need to regroup," Jack said, breaking the silence. "Ivanov is still out there, and we need to figure out his next move before he makes it."

Lisa nodded, her eyes focused. "Agreed. But we can't just wait for him to make the next move. We need to be proactive, find his weak points, and hit him hard."

Sarah, who had been studying a map spread out on the table, looked up. "I think I might have an idea. I've been analyzing the data we recovered from the compound. There are several locations that Ivanov has used as safe houses and meeting points. If we can identify his patterns, we might be able to predict his next move."

Jack leaned over the map, his eyes scanning the various marked locations. "Good. Let's start cross-referencing these locations with any recent activity we've seen. We need to narrow down our options and plan our next strike."

As they worked, the hours ticked by. The atmosphere in the safe house was tense, with the constant hum of the surveillance equipment and the distant sounds of the city providing a backdrop to their intense discussions. The strain of their mission was beginning to take its toll, not just physically but emotionally as well.

As the night wore on, Jack and Lisa took a break, stepping outside to get some fresh air. The cool night breeze was a welcome relief from the stifling tension inside the safe house.

Lisa leaned against the wall, her eyes closed. "This is getting harder every day, Jack. We've been at this for months, and it feels like we're barely making progress."

Jack nodded, his gaze fixed on the distant city lights. "I know. But we can't give up. Ivanov is counting on us to get frustrated and make mistakes. We need to stay focused."

Lisa opened her eyes, looking at Jack with a mixture of admiration and concern. "You've been pushing yourself too hard. We all have. Maybe we need to take a step back and regroup, clear our heads."

Jack sighed, running a hand through his hair. "You're right. But every time we take a step back, Ivanov gets a step ahead. I can't shake the feeling that we're always playing catch-up."

Back inside, Sarah was still poring over the maps and data. She glanced up as Jack and Lisa re-entered, her expression unreadable. "Did you find anything useful?" she asked, her voice betraying a hint of tension.

Jack shook his head. "Not yet. But we need to keep looking. Ivanov's not going to stop, and neither can we."

Sarah nodded, but Jack could see the strain in her eyes. The weight of her dual life as an undercover operative and a detective was beginning to take its toll. She had risked everything to gather the intelligence that had brought them this far, and the pressure was starting to show.

As the night dragged on, the three of them continued to work, their determination unwavering despite the exhaustion that gnawed at them. The safe house, once a place of relative safety and refuge, now felt like a pressure cooker, ready to explode.

Amidst the planning and strategizing, personal dynamics and hidden tensions began to surface. Jack and Lisa's partnership had always been strong, built on mutual respect and trust, but the strain of their mission was starting to fray the edges.

Lisa glanced at Jack, her expression troubled. "Jack, I need to talk to you about something."

Jack looked up from the maps, his brow furrowed. "What is it?"

Lisa hesitated, then took a deep breath. "It's about Sarah. I know she's been invaluable to our mission, but I can't shake the feeling that there's something she's not telling us. Something important."

Jack glanced at Sarah, who was focused on her laptop, then back at Lisa. "What do you mean?"

"I don't know," Lisa admitted. "Maybe it's just the stress getting to me, but I feel like there's more to her story than she's letting on. And with everything that's happened, we can't afford any more surprises."

Jack nodded, his mind racing. He trusted Sarah, but Lisa's concerns were valid. They couldn't afford any more mistakes or secrets. He resolved to talk to Sarah and get to the bottom of it.

Later that night, Jack approached Sarah, who was sitting alone, staring at her screen. "Sarah, can we talk?"

Sarah looked up, her eyes tired but alert. "Sure, Jack. What's on your mind?"

Jack took a seat across from her, his expression serious. "Lisa and I have been talking, and we need to know if there's anything you're not telling us. Anything that could affect our mission."

Sarah's eyes widened slightly, but she quickly composed herself. "I've told you everything I know about Ivanov and his operations. Why do you ask?"

Jack leaned forward, his gaze intense. "Because we're running out of time, and we can't afford any more surprises. If there's anything else, anything at all, we need to know."

Sarah hesitated, her eyes searching Jack's face. Then she sighed, looking down at her hands. "There is something. Something I've been keeping to myself because I wasn't sure how to handle it."

Jack's heart raced. "What is it?"

Sarah looked up, her expression conflicted. "Ivanov isn't just targeting us because we're law enforcement. He's targeting us because he knows us. Personally. He has connections that go back years, connections that tie him to our pasts."

Jack's mind reeled. "What do you mean?"

Sarah took a deep breath. "Ivanov was involved in a covert operation years ago, one that I was a part of before I joined the police force. He knows about my past, and he's using it against us. He knows our weaknesses, our vulnerabilities. And he's not afraid to exploit them."

Jack felt a surge of anger and frustration. "Why didn't you tell us this sooner?"

Sarah's eyes filled with regret. "I didn't know how. I thought I could handle it on my own, but it's become clear that I can't. I'm sorry, Jack. I should have told you."

Jack took a deep breath, trying to calm the storm of emotions swirling inside him. "We can't change the past, Sarah. But we need to stay focused on the mission. We need to use this information to our advantage."

Sarah nodded, her eyes filled with determination. "Agreed. Let's take Ivanov down, once and for all."

As they continued to plan and strategize, the atmosphere in the safe house grew more tense. The personal dynamics and hidden tensions between Jack, Lisa, and Sarah were coming to light, adding another layer of complexity to their mission.

The next day, as they reviewed their plans, the safe house was suddenly rocked by an explosion. The force of the blast threw them to the ground, and the air was filled with smoke and debris.

"Jack! Lisa! Sarah!" Jack shouted, his voice barely audible over the ringing in his ears.

He struggled to his feet, his vision blurred and his ears ringing. He could see Lisa and Sarah nearby, both of them dazed but alive. He rushed to their side, helping them to their feet.

"We need to get out of here," Jack said, his voice urgent. "It's a trap."

They stumbled towards the exit, the sound of gunfire echoing through the building. The syndicate had found them, and they were under attack. Jack's mind raced as he tried to think of a way out.

As they reached the door, they were confronted by a group of heavily armed men. Jack and Lisa drew their weapons, returning fire as they fought their way through the attackers. Sarah provided cover fire, her sharpshooting skills proving invaluable.

Despite their efforts, the situation was dire. The syndicate had the upper hand, and they were outnumbered and outgunned. Jack's heart pounded with fear and frustration as he realized they might not make it out alive.

In the midst of the chaos, a familiar figure appeared – Ivanov. He stood at the edge of the room, his cold, calculating smile sending a chill down Jack's spine.

"Detective Thompson," Ivanov said, his voice smooth and unflappable. "I must admit, I'm impressed. You've been a worthy adversary. But this ends now."

Jack's eyes narrowed. "It's over, Ivanov. Surrender now, and no one else has to get hurt."

Ivanov's smile widened. "You think you can stop me? You have no idea what you're up against."

Before Jack could react, Ivanov activated a hidden switch, and the room filled with a blinding flash of light. Jack and Lisa were thrown to the ground, their senses overwhelmed by the sudden explosion.

When the dust settled, Ivanov and his men were gone, leaving behind a scene of destruction. Jack struggled to his feet, his ears ringing and his vision blurred.

"Lisa, are you okay?" he called out, his voice strained.

Lisa groaned, pushing herself up from the debris. "Yeah, I'm fine. But Ivanov got away."

Jack's frustration boiled over. "Damn it! We were so close."

Sarah joined them, her expression grim. "We need to regroup. Ivanov's still out there, and he won't stop until he's achieved his goals."

They quickly secured the safe house, assessing the damage and tending to their wounds. Despite the attack, they were determined to continue their mission.

Back at the precinct, Jack, Lisa, and Sarah reviewed the evidence they had collected. Among the documents were detailed plans for the assassinations and kidnappings Ivanov had been orchestrating. They also found a list of names – key figures in law enforcement and politics who were targeted by the syndicate.

"We need to warn these people," Lisa said, her voice urgent. "They're in grave danger."

Jack nodded. "Agreed. We also need to continue our pursuit of Ivanov. He's not going to stop, and neither can we."

Over the next few days, they worked tirelessly to protect the individuals on Ivanov's hit list, coordinating with local and federal authorities to provide security and thwart any assassination attempts. Their efforts paid off, and several high-profile targets were saved from imminent danger.

Meanwhile, they continued their pursuit of Ivanov, following every lead and scrutinizing every piece of evidence. It was a grueling process, but they were determined to see it through.

One evening, as they pored over the latest intelligence reports, Sarah made a startling discovery. Hidden within the documents they had recovered from the safe house was a coded message – a message that hinted at a larger conspiracy.

"Jack, Lisa, look at this," Sarah said, pointing to the screen. "I think this message is from Ivanov. It mentions something called 'Operation Phoenix.'"

Jack's eyes narrowed. "Operation Phoenix? What is that?"

Sarah began decoding the message, her fingers flying across the keyboard. "From what I can gather, it's a plan to destabilize the city by targeting critical infrastructure – power plants, water supply, transportation networks. Ivanov's trying to create chaos on a massive scale."

Lisa's expression hardened. "We need to stop this. If Ivanov succeeds, it could be catastrophic."

Jack agreed. "We need to find out where and when this is going to happen. We can't let Ivanov execute his plan."

They spent the next few hours deciphering the message and analyzing the data. It was a race against time, but their efforts paid off. They discovered that Ivanov was planning to launch Operation Phoenix in three days, using a series of coordinated attacks to bring the city to its knees.

Armed with this knowledge, they mobilized their forces, coordinating with local and federal agencies to prevent the attacks. The city was placed on high alert, and security was heightened at all critical infrastructure sites.

As the day of the planned attacks approached, the tension was palpable. Jack, Lisa, and Sarah worked around the clock, monitoring the situation and coordinating their response.

Finally, the day arrived. The city was on edge, but they were ready. Jack and Lisa led the main response team, while Sarah provided crucial intelligence from their command center.

As they monitored the situation, they received word that Ivanov had been spotted near one of the power plants. Jack's heart raced. This was their chance to capture him and put an end to his plans.

"Let's move," Jack ordered, leading his team to the location.

They arrived at the power plant, where they found Ivanov and his men preparing to launch their attack. The air was thick with tension as they approached, their weapons at the ready.

"Drop your weapons!" Jack shouted, his voice echoing through the facility.

Ivanov turned to face them, a cold smile playing on his lips. "Ah, Detective Thompson. Right on time."

The firefight erupted, the sound of gunfire echoing through the plant. Jack and Lisa fought with precision and determination, their every move calculated. Sarah provided crucial intelligence, guiding them through the chaos.

Despite the intense battle, Ivanov remained a formidable adversary. He moved with the precision of a trained soldier, his every action calculated and deadly.

As the fight raged on, Jack finally managed to corner Ivanov. Their eyes locked, and Jack felt a surge of determination.

"It's over, Ivanov," Jack growled. "You're done."

Ivanov's smile never wavered. "You think you've won, Detective? This is just the beginning."

Before Jack could react, Ivanov activated a hidden detonator, triggering a series of explosions. The facility shook, and Jack was thrown to the ground.

When the dust settled, Ivanov was gone, leaving behind a trail of destruction. Jack struggled to his feet, his mind racing.

"Lisa, are you okay?" he called out.

Lisa groaned, pushing herself up from the debris. "Yeah, I'm fine. But Ivanov escaped."

Jack's frustration boiled over. "Damn it! We were so close."

Sarah's voice crackled over the radio. "Jack, we need to regroup. There's more at stake here than we realized."

Jack and Lisa made their way back to the command center, where they reviewed the latest intelligence. They discovered that Ivanov's escape was part of a larger conspiracy – a network of criminal organizations working together to destabilize the city.

"We're dealing with something much bigger than we thought," Sarah said, her voice filled with determination. "We need to keep digging, keep fighting."

Jack nodded, his resolve unwavering. "Agreed. Ivanov may have escaped, but we won't stop until we've brought him and his entire network to justice."

Over the next few weeks, they continued their pursuit of Ivanov, following every lead and scrutinizing every piece of evidence. The battle was far from over, but they were more determined than ever to see it through.

One evening, as they worked late in the precinct, Jack received an unexpected call. The voice on the other end was familiar – it was the anonymous source who had provided them with crucial information in the past.

"Detective Thompson," the voice said, "I have information about Ivanov's next move. He's planning something big, and you need to be ready."

"What is he planning?" Jack asked, his voice filled with urgency.

"I can't say much, but it's going to happen soon. Be prepared," the voice replied before hanging up.

With the ominous warning hanging over them, Jack, Lisa, and Sarah knew they needed to stay vigilant. The fight against Ivanov and his network was far from over, but they were ready for whatever came their way.

As the sun set over Bay City, casting a golden glow over the skyline, Jack felt a renewed sense of purpose. The battle against Ivanov was a long and arduous one, but he knew they had the strength and determination to see it through.

The future was uncertain, and the challenges ahead were daunting. But with Lisa and Sarah by his side, Jack knew they could face whatever came their way. The fight for Bay City had only just begun, and they were prepared to see it through to the end.

With each step they took, they moved closer to reclaiming their city from the grip of Ivanov and his network. The battle was far from over, but they were ready for whatever lay ahead. The shadows of betrayal and corruption loomed large, but they knew that together, they could overcome any obstacle.

The fight for Bay City was their mission, their purpose, and they would not rest until justice was served. As the night settled over the city, Jack, Lisa, and Sarah stood ready, prepared to face whatever challenges lay ahead. The future was uncertain, but their resolve was unbreakable. The battle for Bay City had only just begun, and they were prepared to see it through to the end.

Chapter 12: The Inside Job

The tension in the precinct was palpable as Sarah Miller paced back and forth, her mind racing. She had been deep undercover within the syndicate for months, gathering crucial intelligence that had helped Jack and Lisa get closer to bringing down the criminal organization. But now, everything was falling apart. She had just received word that her cover had been blown. Her heart pounded with fear and adrenaline as she prepared to make her next move.

Sarah grabbed her phone and dialed Jack's number. He answered on the second ring, his voice tense.

"Jack, it's Sarah. My cover's been blown. They know who I am."

There was a moment of stunned silence on the other end of the line before Jack spoke again, his voice urgent. "Where are you? Are you safe?"

"I'm at my apartment, but I don't know how long I have. They could be coming for me any minute."

"We're on our way. Stay put and stay safe," Jack ordered.

Sarah hung up the phone and took a deep breath, trying to calm her nerves. She had known the risks when she agreed to go undercover, but the reality of the situation was far more terrifying than she had anticipated. She quickly packed a bag with essential items and weapons, preparing for the possibility of having to make a quick escape.

But she didn't get the chance. The sound of a door being kicked in echoed through her apartment, followed by the heavy footsteps of several men. Sarah barely had time to react before they were upon her, guns drawn and faces twisted with anger.

"Drop the bag and put your hands up," one of the men barked.

Sarah complied, knowing that resistance was futile. She recognized the leader of the group as Viktor Ivanov, one of the syndicate's top enforcers. His eyes burned with fury as he approached her, his gun trained on her head.

"You thought you could betray us and get away with it?" Viktor snarled. "You're coming with us."

They bound her hands and blindfolded her, dragging her out of the apartment and into a waiting van. Sarah's mind raced as she tried to think of a way to escape, but the odds were against her. She could only hope that Jack and Lisa would find her before it was too late.

AT THE PRECINCT, JACK and Lisa were already mobilizing their team. The news of Sarah's compromised cover had hit them hard, and they knew they had to act quickly to rescue her.

"Sarah's been taken," Jack said, his voice filled with urgency. "We need to find out where they've taken her and get her back."

Lisa nodded, her expression grim. "We'll need to infiltrate the syndicate's operations. We can't go in guns blazing; we need to be smart about this."

They gathered their most trusted officers and began planning the operation. Their first step was to gather intelligence on the syndicate's safe houses and operational bases. They reached out to their informants, combed through surveillance footage, and analyzed recent communications to pinpoint possible locations where Sarah might be held.

As the hours ticked by, they finally got a break. One of their informants, a low-level syndicate member named Tommy, came forward with information about a safe house on the outskirts of the city. It was heavily guarded and used for high-value hostages and sensitive operations. Jack and Lisa knew it was their best shot at finding Sarah.

They assembled a team and briefed them on the mission. The plan was to infiltrate the safe house under the guise of being new recruits for the syndicate. It was a risky move, but it was the only way to get close without raising suspicion.

THE NIGHT WAS DARK and foreboding as Jack, Lisa, and their team approached the safe house. They were dressed in plain clothes, blending in with the surroundings. The building was an old, abandoned warehouse, its windows boarded up and its exterior covered in graffiti. Guards patrolled the perimeter, their expressions vigilant and hostile.

Jack and Lisa exchanged a glance, their eyes reflecting the high stakes of the mission. They knew they had to play their roles perfectly to avoid detection.

"Stay sharp," Jack whispered to his team. "Follow my lead."

They approached the main entrance, where a guard stopped them, his hand resting on his gun.

"Who are you?" the guard demanded.

Jack stepped forward, his demeanor confident. "We're the new recruits. Tommy sent us."

The guard eyed them suspiciously but nodded. "Alright. Follow me."

They were led into the warehouse, where the air was thick with tension. The interior was dimly lit, with crates and equipment scattered around. Jack and Lisa scanned the area, their senses on high alert.

"Stay close," Jack whispered to Lisa. "We need to find Sarah."

They were led to a central room, where several high-ranking syndicate members were gathered, including Viktor Ivanov. The atmosphere was charged with hostility as Viktor eyed the newcomers.

"New recruits, huh?" Viktor said, his voice dripping with skepticism. "Let's see what you're made of."

He signaled for one of his men to bring in a target – a bound and gagged man who had betrayed the syndicate. Viktor handed Jack a gun.

"Prove your loyalty. Kill him."

Jack's heart raced as he took the gun, his mind racing for a way out. He knew he couldn't kill an innocent man, but he also knew that refusing would blow their cover.

"We can't afford to blow our cover," Lisa whispered, her eyes filled with urgency.

Jack nodded subtly, then took a deep breath. He aimed the gun at the man but fired a shot into the air at the last second, the bullet striking a light fixture overhead. The room was plunged into darkness, and chaos erupted.

"Now!" Jack shouted, and their team sprang into action.

They moved swiftly through the darkness, taking down syndicate members with precision and efficiency. Jack and Lisa led the charge, their movements coordinated and deadly.

"Find Sarah!" Jack shouted, his voice barely audible over the chaos.

Lisa nodded and split off from the group, searching the rooms for any sign of Sarah. She moved quickly, her heart pounding with fear and determination.

Meanwhile, Jack confronted Viktor, their eyes locking in a deadly standoff.

"You've made a big mistake coming here," Viktor sneered, raising his gun.

"You're the one who made a mistake," Jack retorted, lunging at Viktor.

The two men grappled in the darkness, their struggle intense and brutal. Jack's training and determination gave him the edge, and he managed to disarm Viktor and knock him to the ground.

"Where's Sarah?" Jack demanded, his voice filled with fury.

Viktor laughed, blood trickling from his mouth. "You'll never find her in time."

Jack tightened his grip on Viktor, his voice cold. "Watch me."

He left Viktor restrained and continued searching for Sarah, his mind racing with fear and determination. He knew time was running out, and every second counted.

Meanwhile, Lisa finally found Sarah in a back room, bound and gagged but alive. She quickly freed her, her eyes filled with relief.

"Sarah, thank God," Lisa said, helping her to her feet.

"Jack, Viktor's here," Sarah said urgently. "We need to get out of here. Now."

They rejoined Jack, who had just finished securing the remaining syndicate members. The team moved quickly, making their way to the exit. But as they reached the door, they were confronted by a new wave of syndicate reinforcements.

"We're not out of the woods yet," Jack said, his voice filled with determination. "Stay sharp."

The firefight was intense, the air filled with the sound of gunfire and the acrid smell of gunpowder. Jack, Lisa, and Sarah fought with precision and determination, their every move calculated.

Despite the chaos, they managed to break through the reinforcements and make their way to their vehicle. They sped away from the warehouse, their hearts pounding with relief and adrenaline.

As they drove back to the precinct, the reality of the night's events began to sink in. They had rescued Sarah, but the battle was far from over. The syndicate was a formidable foe, and they knew that their retaliation would be swift and brutal.

BACK AT THE PRECINCT, Sarah was debriefed and given medical attention. She was shaken but determined to continue the fight.

"We need to regroup and plan our next move," Jack said, his voice filled with resolve. "The syndicate won't stop until we're all dead."

Lisa nodded. "We'll take the fight to them. But we need to be smart about it."

Over the next few days, they worked tirelessly to gather intelligence and strategize their next move. They knew that Viktor and the syndicate wouldn't rest until they were neutralized, and they needed to stay one step ahead.

As they prepared for their next operation, they received a message from a new informant – a high-ranking syndicate member who was willing to defect in exchange for protection.

"Meet me at the old factory on Fifth Street. Midnight. Come alone," the message read.

Jack and Lisa exchanged a glance, their minds racing. It was a risky move, but it was also an opportunity they couldn't afford to pass up.

"We'll go," Jack said. "But we'll need backup nearby, just in case."

Lisa nodded. "Agreed. Let's do this."

THE OLD FACTORY WAS dark and foreboding as Jack and Lisa approached, their senses on high alert. They knew the risks, but they also knew that this informant could provide the breakthrough they needed.

As they entered the building, they saw a figure standing in the shadows. The informant stepped forward, his face partially obscured by a hood.

"Detective Thompson, Detective Ramirez," the informant said, his voice low. "Thank you for coming."

"Who are you?" Jack asked, his voice cautious.

"I'm Alexei Petrov," the informant replied, lowering his hood. "I'm one of Viktor's lieutenants. But I've had enough. I want out."

Jack and Lisa exchanged a glance, their minds racing. They knew they needed to tread carefully.

"Why now?" Lisa asked. "Why defect?"

"Viktor's gone too far," Alexei said, his voice filled with frustration. "He's planning something big, something that will destroy this city. I can't be a part of it anymore."

Jack's eyes narrowed. "What is he planning?"

Alexei handed them a folder. "Everything you need to know is in here. Locations, names, plans. But you need to act fast. Viktor's already moving."

Jack took the folder, his mind racing. "Thank you. We'll protect you, but you need to stay hidden."

Alexei nodded. "I understand. Good luck."

BACK AT THE PRECINCT, Jack and Lisa reviewed the information in the folder. It was a goldmine of intelligence, detailing Viktor's plans for a massive attack on the city's infrastructure.

"This is it," Jack said, his voice filled with determination. "We have to stop him."

They mobilized their team and coordinated with their allies in the DEA and the FBI. The goal was to intercept Viktor and prevent the attack before it could happen.

As night fell, they moved out, their hearts pounding with anticipation. The location was a sprawling industrial complex on the outskirts of the city, a place that was both heavily guarded and strategically important.

Jack, Lisa, and Sarah led the main assault team, while Agents Morgan and Bennett coordinated from a mobile command center. They approached the complex under the cover of darkness, their movements silent and coordinated.

"Stay sharp," Jack whispered to his team. "We move in on my signal."

They crept forward, using the shadows for cover. As they neared the entrance, they saw the syndicate members patrolling the perimeter. Jack signaled for Lisa to take the lead, and they moved in quickly, taking out the guards with precision and efficiency.

Inside, the complex was a maze of corridors and rooms, filled with syndicate members going about their business. The team moved swiftly, neutralizing threats and securing the area as they advanced.

As they approached the central command room, Jack's senses were on high alert. The air was thick with tension, and every sound seemed amplified.

"Sarah, you take the left," Jack instructed. "Lisa and I will cover the right. Let's move."

They breached the command room, taking down the guards with precision and efficiency. In the center of the room stood Viktor, his expression cold and calculating.

"You're too late," Viktor sneered, raising his gun.

Jack and Lisa moved quickly, disarming Viktor and restraining him. The tension in the room was palpable as they confronted him.

"Tell us everything," Jack demanded, his voice filled with fury.

Viktor laughed, a chilling sound. "You think you can stop us? This is just the beginning."

Jack tightened his grip on Viktor, his voice cold. "Watch us."

With Viktor in custody and the syndicate members either captured or neutralized, the operation was a success. They gathered evidence from the complex, uncovering a cache of weapons and plans that would prove invaluable in their ongoing investigation.

As they regrouped at the mobile command center, the sense of victory was tempered by the knowledge that the battle was far from over. The syndicate was a formidable foe, and they knew that their retaliation would be swift and brutal.

Agent Morgan approached, her expression serious. "Good work tonight. But we need to stay on our guard. The syndicate won't take this lying down."

Agent Bennett added, "We've made significant progress, but we need to keep the pressure on. The more we disrupt their operations, the more desperate they'll become."

Jack nodded, his resolve unwavering. "Agreed. We're in this for the long haul. We can't afford to let up now."

Over the next few weeks, the coalition of law enforcement agencies continued their efforts to dismantle the syndicate. They conducted raids, intercepted shipments, and gathered intelligence, all while keeping a close watch on their new allies.

The uneasy alliance with Alexei proved to be both a blessing and a curse. While his information was invaluable, the tension between the two groups remained high. Trust was a fragile commodity, and both sides knew that betrayal was always a possibility.

As they continued their work, Jack felt a renewed sense of purpose. The fight against the syndicate was far from over, but he knew they had the strength and determination to see it through.

The future was uncertain, and the challenges ahead were daunting. But with Lisa and Sarah by his side, Jack knew they could face whatever came their way. The fight for Bay City had only just begun, and they were prepared to see it through to the end.

With each step they took, they moved closer to reclaiming their city from the grip of the syndicate. The battle was far from over, but they were ready for whatever lay ahead. The shadows of betrayal and corruption loomed large, but they knew that together, they could overcome any obstacle.

The fight for Bay City was their mission, their purpose, and they would not rest until justice was served. As the night settled over the city, Jack, Lisa, and Sarah stood ready, prepared to face whatever challenges lay ahead. The future was uncertain, but their resolve was unbreakable. The battle for Bay City had only just begun, and they were prepared to see it through to the end.

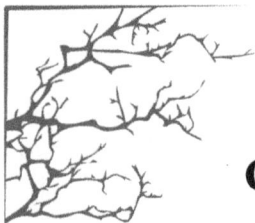

Chapter 13: The Final Countdown

Jack Thompson sat at his desk, his eyes fixed on the map spread out before him. The recent intel they had gathered pointed to one horrifying conclusion: The Wolf's ultimate plan was to destabilize Bay City in a catastrophic way. This plan would be the syndicate's final stand, an act of desperation that would leave the city in ruins if successful. The implications were chilling, and the urgency of the situation weighed heavily on Jack's shoulders.

Lisa Ramirez entered the room, her expression grim. "Jack, we've just intercepted another message. It's bad. The Wolf is planning to hit multiple targets across the city simultaneously."

Jack looked up, his eyes reflecting the severity of the situation. "What are the targets?"

Lisa handed him a list. "The power grid, the water supply, and the main transportation hub. If they succeed, it will cripple the city."

Jack's mind raced. "We need to act fast. We can't let them succeed. Get everyone together. We're going to need all the help we can get."

As Lisa moved to gather their team, Jack picked up his phone and called Sarah Miller. She had been recovering from her ordeal, but he knew they needed her expertise now more than ever.

"Sarah, it's Jack. We've got a situation. The Wolf is planning to take down the city. We need you."

Sarah's voice was steady despite the gravity of the situation. "I'm on my way."

Jack then reached out to their allies in the DEA and the FBI, coordinating a joint operation that would be their most ambitious yet. Special Agent Rachel Morgan and Agent Tom Bennett were quick to respond, understanding the critical nature of the mission.

By the time everyone had assembled in the war room, the tension was palpable. Jack stood at the head of the table, his expression serious as he addressed the group.

"Alright, everyone. We have intel that The Wolf is planning a coordinated attack to cripple Bay City. Our targets are the power grid, the water supply, and the transportation hub. We need to divide our forces and hit all three locations simultaneously. This is it – our final assault to bring down the syndicate once and for all."

Agent Morgan stepped forward. "The FBI will take the transportation hub. We have the resources and the manpower to handle it."

Agent Bennett nodded. "The DEA will secure the water supply. We've got a team ready to move out."

Jack turned to his own team. "That leaves us with the power grid. It's going to be heavily guarded, but we have to secure it. If they take it down, the whole city goes dark."

Lisa spoke up, her voice filled with determination. "We've got this, Jack. We'll take them down."

The team spent the next few hours planning their assault, coordinating with their allies and ensuring that every detail was covered. They knew that failure was not an option. As the clock ticked down, the weight of their mission settled heavily on their shoulders.

NIGHT FELL OVER BAY City, shrouding it in a tense silence. The team moved out, their hearts pounding with anticipation. Jack, Lisa, and Sarah led the assault on the power grid, while Agents Morgan and Bennett moved to their respective targets.

The power grid facility was a sprawling complex on the outskirts of the city, surrounded by high fences and patrolled by heavily armed guards. The team approached under the cover of darkness, their movements silent and coordinated.

"Stay sharp," Jack whispered. "We move in on my signal."

They crept forward, using the shadows for cover. As they neared the entrance, they saw the guards patrolling the perimeter. Jack signaled for Lisa to take the lead, and they moved in quickly, taking out the guards with precision and efficiency.

Inside, the facility was a maze of corridors and control rooms, filled with the hum of machinery and the glow of computer screens. The team moved swiftly, neutralizing threats and securing the area as they advanced.

"Sarah, you take the left," Jack instructed. "Lisa and I will cover the right. Let's move."

They split up, each team navigating the labyrinthine interior of the facility. Jack and Lisa moved with practiced ease, their senses on high alert.

As they approached the central control room, they encountered a group of syndicate members. A firefight erupted, the air filled with the deafening sound of gunfire and the acrid smell of gunpowder. Jack and Lisa fought with precision and determination, their every move calculated.

"Cover me!" Jack shouted, advancing towards the control room.

Lisa provided cover fire, her aim steady and true. Jack moved quickly, taking down the remaining syndicate members and securing the control room.

"We've got it," Jack said, his voice filled with relief. "Now we just need to secure the main generator."

They moved towards the generator room, their senses on high alert. As they entered, they were confronted by a familiar figure – Viktor Ivanov, standing with a group of heavily armed men.

"You're too late," Viktor sneered. "The Wolf's plan is already in motion."

Jack's eyes narrowed. "We'll see about that."

A fierce battle ensued, the room filled with the sounds of gunfire and the clash of metal. Jack and Lisa fought with unrelenting determination, their every move driven by the urgency of their mission.

In the midst of the chaos, Sarah managed to slip past the guards and reach the control panel. She quickly began working to override the system and shut down the countdown timer.

"I've got this," Sarah shouted, her fingers flying over the keyboard.

Jack and Lisa continued to hold off the syndicate members, their focus unwavering. Viktor fought with a brutal intensity, but Jack's determination gave him the edge. He managed to disarm Viktor and knock him to the ground.

"You're finished," Jack growled, restraining Viktor.

Viktor laughed, a chilling sound. "You think you can stop us? This is just the beginning."

Jack tightened his grip, his voice cold. "We'll see about that."

With Viktor restrained and the remaining syndicate members either captured or neutralized, the team focused on securing the generator. Sarah worked quickly, her hands steady despite the high stakes.

"I've got it," Sarah said, her voice filled with relief. "The countdown is stopped. The power grid is secure."

Jack and Lisa exchanged a look of relief, their hearts still pounding with adrenaline. They had done it – they had stopped The Wolf's plan to take down the power grid.

"Good work," Jack said, his voice filled with pride. "Let's regroup with the others and make sure the other targets are secure."

AT THE TRANSPORTATION hub, Agent Morgan and her team moved with precision, securing the area and neutralizing the syndicate members. The hub was a critical point for the city's infrastructure, and they knew they had to prevent any disruptions.

"Secure the entrances," Agent Morgan ordered, her voice steady. "We need to make sure no one gets in or out."

The team moved swiftly, their training and coordination evident in every move. They encountered heavy resistance, but their determination and skill saw them through.

As they reached the central control room, they found a group of syndicate members attempting to sabotage the system. A fierce firefight ensued, but Agent Morgan's team managed to overpower them and secure the area.

"The transportation hub is secure," Agent Morgan reported, her voice filled with relief. "We're good here."

AT THE WATER SUPPLY facility, Agent Bennett and his team faced similar challenges. The facility was a sprawling complex, and the syndicate had fortified their positions, ready for a fight.

"Move in," Agent Bennett ordered, leading the charge.

The team advanced quickly, neutralizing threats and securing the area as they moved. They encountered heavy resistance, but their training and determination saw them through.

As they reached the main control room, they found a group of syndicate members attempting to sabotage the system. A fierce firefight ensued, but Agent Bennett's team managed to overpower them and secure the area.

"The water supply is secure," Agent Bennett reported, his voice filled with relief. "We're good here."

BACK AT THE POWER GRID facility, Jack, Lisa, and Sarah regrouped with their team, their hearts still pounding with adrenaline. They had stopped The Wolf's plan, but they knew the battle was far from over.

"Good work, everyone," Jack said, his voice filled with pride. "We've secured the targets, but we need to stay vigilant. The syndicate won't take this lying down."

Lisa nodded, her expression serious. "Agreed. We need to be ready for anything."

As they prepared to leave the facility, Jack received a call from Agent Morgan. "Jack, we've got a lead on The Wolf's location. He's at a safe house in the city. We need to move now."

Jack's heart raced. "We're on our way."

They quickly coordinated with their allies and moved out, their hearts pounding with anticipation. The safe house was located in a secluded part of the city, heavily guarded and fortified.

As they approached, Jack's senses were on high alert. The air was thick with tension, and every shadow seemed to conceal a potential threat.

"Stay sharp," Jack whispered to his team. "We move in on my signal."

They crept forward, using the shadows for cover. As they neared the entrance, they saw the guards patrolling the perimeter. Jack signaled for Lisa to take the lead, and they moved in quickly, taking out the guards with precision and efficiency.

Inside, the safe house was a maze of corridors and rooms, filled with syndicate members going about their business. The team moved swiftly, neutralizing threats and securing the area as they advanced.

As they approached the central command room, they encountered a group of heavily armed syndicate members. A fierce firefight erupted, the air filled with the deafening sound of

gunfire and the acrid smell of gunpowder. Jack and Lisa fought with precision and determination, their every move calculated.

"Cover me!" Jack shouted, advancing towards the command room.

Lisa provided cover fire, her aim steady and true. Jack moved quickly, taking down the remaining syndicate members and securing the command room.

In the center of the room stood The Wolf, his expression cold and calculating.

"You're too late," The Wolf sneered, raising his gun.

Jack and Lisa moved quickly, disarming The Wolf and restraining him. The tension in the room was palpable as they confronted him.

"Tell us everything," Jack demanded, his voice filled with fury.

The Wolf laughed, a chilling sound. "You think you can stop us? This is just the beginning."

Jack tightened his grip, his voice cold. "We'll see about that."

With The Wolf in custody and the remaining syndicate members either captured or neutralized, the operation was a success. They gathered evidence from the safe house, uncovering a cache of weapons and plans that would prove invaluable in their ongoing investigation.

As they regrouped at the mobile command center, the sense of victory was tempered by the knowledge that the battle was far from over. The syndicate was a formidable foe, and they knew that their retaliation would be swift and brutal.

Agent Morgan approached, her expression serious. "Good work tonight. But we need to stay on our guard. The syndicate won't take this lying down."

Agent Bennett added, "We've made significant progress, but we need to keep the pressure on. The more we disrupt their operations, the more desperate they'll become."

Jack nodded, his resolve unwavering. "Agreed. We're in this for the long haul. We can't afford to let up now."

Over the next few weeks, the coalition of law enforcement agencies continued their efforts to dismantle the syndicate. They conducted raids, intercepted shipments, and gathered intelligence, all while keeping a close watch on their new allies.

The uneasy alliance with Alexei Petrov proved to be both a blessing and a curse. While his information was invaluable, the tension between the two groups remained high. Trust was a fragile commodity, and both sides knew that betrayal was always a possibility.

As they continued their work, Jack felt a renewed sense of purpose. The fight against the syndicate was far from over, but he knew they had the strength and determination to see it through.

The future was uncertain, and the challenges ahead were daunting. But with Lisa and Sarah by his side, Jack knew they could face whatever came their way. The fight for Bay City had only just begun, and they were prepared to see it through to the end.

With each step they took, they moved closer to reclaiming their city from the grip of the syndicate. The battle was far from over, but they were ready for whatever lay ahead. The shadows of betrayal and corruption loomed large, but they knew that together, they could overcome any obstacle.

The fight for Bay City was their mission, their purpose, and they would not rest until justice was served. As the night settled over the city, Jack, Lisa, and Sarah stood ready, prepared to face whatever challenges lay ahead. The future was uncertain, but their resolve was unbreakable. The battle for Bay City had only just begun, and they were prepared to see it through to the end.

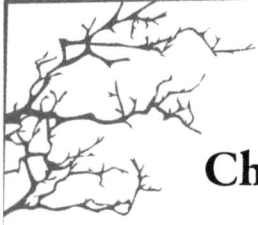

Chapter 14: Showdown at Midnight

The cityscape of Bay City was bathed in the soft glow of twilight as the clock neared midnight. Jack Thompson stood in the war room, surrounded by his team, as they prepared for what would be their final assault on the syndicate's central hub. This was it – the culmination of months of relentless pursuit, grueling battles, and countless sacrifices. The syndicate's central hub was a fortress-like compound situated on the outskirts of the city, heavily guarded and fortified with the latest security measures. It was the heart of their operations, and tonight, Jack and his team would storm it in a bid to dismantle the syndicate once and for all.

Jack addressed the room, his voice steady and commanding. "This is it, everyone. The final push. We've fought hard to get here, and now we have a chance to end this. The Wolf is in that compound, and we're going to bring him down. Stay focused, stay sharp, and watch each other's backs. Let's finish this."

Detective Lisa Ramirez stood beside him, her expression resolute. "We know what's at stake. We're ready."

Sarah Miller, still recovering from her ordeal but determined to see this through, nodded. "Let's bring The Wolf down."

Special Agent Rachel Morgan and Agent Tom Bennett from the FBI and DEA were also present, their teams ready to support the operation. Their combined forces would ensure they had the firepower and strategic advantage needed to breach the compound.

The plan was meticulously laid out. They would divide into three teams, each assigned a specific entry point to breach the compound simultaneously. The element of surprise was crucial, and they had to move swiftly to neutralize the guards and secure the central command center where The Wolf was believed to be located.

As the teams geared up and checked their equipment, Jack took a moment to gather his thoughts. This was the most critical operation of his career, and the lives of his team depended on its success. He knew the risks, but he also knew they had come too far to turn back now.

The convoy of unmarked vehicles moved through the darkened streets of Bay City, their headlights off to avoid detection. The tension in the air was palpable, each member of the team acutely aware of the danger they were about to face. As they approached the compound, the vehicles stopped a safe distance away, and the teams disembarked, moving swiftly and silently towards their designated entry points.

Jack led Team Alpha, which included Lisa, Sarah, and a group of highly trained officers. Their objective was to breach the main entrance and secure the central courtyard. Agent Morgan led Team Bravo, tasked with securing the perimeter and neutralizing any external threats. Agent Bennett's Team Charlie would breach the rear entrance and move towards the command center from the opposite side, trapping The Wolf in a pincer maneuver.

"Positions," Jack whispered into his earpiece, signaling the teams to move into position.

They moved like shadows through the night, their steps silent and purposeful. The compound loomed ahead, a dark silhouette against the night sky. The main entrance was guarded by a pair of heavily armed sentries, their expressions vigilant.

"On my mark," Jack whispered to his team. "Three... two... one... Mark!"

Simultaneously, the teams breached their respective entry points. Jack and Lisa took out the sentries with swift, silent precision, moving into the compound's courtyard. The element of surprise was on their side, and they advanced quickly, neutralizing guards and securing the area.

Gunfire erupted as the guards inside the compound realized they were under attack. The air was filled with the deafening sound of bullets and the acrid smell of gunpowder. Jack and his team moved with practiced efficiency, their training and determination guiding their every move.

"Bravo team, perimeter secure," Agent Morgan's voice crackled over the radio. "Moving in."

"Charlie team, rear entrance breached," Agent Bennett reported. "Advancing towards the command center."

Jack and Lisa led their team through the courtyard, advancing towards the main building. The compound was a maze of corridors and rooms, and they moved swiftly, clearing each one as they advanced.

As they approached the central command center, they encountered a group of heavily armed syndicate members. A fierce firefight erupted, the air thick with tension and danger. Jack and Lisa fought side by side, their movements fluid and synchronized.

"Cover me!" Jack shouted, advancing towards the command center door.

Lisa provided cover fire, her aim steady and precise. Jack moved quickly, taking down the remaining guards and securing the entrance. They regrouped with Sarah and the rest of the team, ready to breach the final door.

"This is it," Jack said, his voice filled with determination. "We take The Wolf down, once and for all."

They breached the door, storming into the command center. The room was filled with high-tech equipment, monitors displaying various feeds from around the compound. In the center of the room stood The Wolf, his expression cold and calculating.

"You're too late," The Wolf sneered, his eyes filled with malice. "You think you can stop me?"

Jack leveled his gun at The Wolf, his voice steady. "It's over. Surrender now."

The Wolf laughed, a chilling sound that echoed through the room. "You have no idea what you're dealing with. This is just the beginning."

Before Jack could respond, The Wolf pressed a button on a device he held in his hand. Alarms blared, and the monitors flashed red. The compound was rigged with explosives, and they were running out of time.

"Get down!" Jack shouted, diving for cover as the first explosion rocked the building.

The command center was engulfed in chaos as the team scrambled to find cover. Jack and Lisa managed to shield Sarah as debris rained down around them. The Wolf used the chaos to his advantage, slipping away through a hidden exit.

"We have to stop him!" Jack shouted, his voice barely audible over the noise. "Lisa, Sarah, with me!"

They pursued The Wolf through the maze of corridors, the building shaking with each successive explosion. The compound was a death trap, and they knew they had to move quickly.

"Bravo team, Charlie team, the compound is rigged with explosives!" Jack radioed. "Evacuate immediately!"

"We're on it," Agent Morgan responded. "We'll cover your escape."

Jack, Lisa, and Sarah continued their pursuit, following The Wolf through the labyrinthine interior of the compound. They emerged into a large, open warehouse area, where The Wolf had taken cover behind a stack of crates.

"End of the line, Wolf!" Jack shouted, advancing with his gun drawn.

The Wolf stood, his expression defiant. "You can't stop me. The syndicate will rise again, stronger than ever."

Jack's eyes narrowed. "Not if I have anything to say about it."

A final, intense firefight erupted as Jack, Lisa, and Sarah engaged The Wolf and his remaining guards. The stakes were higher than ever, and the air was thick with the sound of gunfire and the acrid smell of smoke.

Jack moved with precision and determination, his every action guided by the need to bring The Wolf to justice. Lisa and Sarah provided cover, their teamwork and coordination honed by months of working together.

As the last of The Wolf's guards fell, Jack advanced on The Wolf, his gun trained on the syndicate leader.

"It's over," Jack said, his voice filled with resolve. "Surrender now."

The Wolf sneered, his eyes filled with hatred. "You think you've won? You've only delayed the inevitable."

Jack tightened his grip on his gun. "We'll see about that."

Before The Wolf could respond, a final explosion rocked the building, the force of the blast knocking everyone off their feet. The warehouse was engulfed in flames, and the structure began to collapse.

"Get out! Now!" Jack shouted, helping Lisa and Sarah to their feet.

They scrambled towards the exit, the building collapsing around them. The heat was intense, and the air was filled with smoke and debris. Jack, Lisa, and Sarah managed to reach the exit just as the warehouse collapsed in a fiery inferno.

They emerged into the cool night air, coughing and gasping for breath. The compound was in ruins, a testament to the devastation wrought by The Wolf's final act of defiance.

Agent Morgan and Agent Bennett met them outside, their expressions filled with relief.

"Is it over?" Agent Morgan asked, her voice hopeful.

Jack nodded, his eyes filled with determination. "The Wolf is dead. The syndicate is finished."

As they regrouped with their teams, the reality of their victory began to sink in. They had dismantled the syndicate, brought down its leader, and saved Bay City from a catastrophic fate.

IN THE DAYS THAT FOLLOWED, the news of the syndicate's downfall spread throughout Bay City. The city began to heal, the scars of the battle a reminder of the price of justice. Jack, Lisa, and Sarah were hailed as heroes, their efforts recognized and celebrated by their colleagues and the community.

But for Jack, the victory was bittersweet. The fight had taken a toll, and he knew that the battle against crime and corruption would never truly be over. Yet, he also knew that they had made a difference, that their actions had brought hope and safety to a city that had been on the brink of destruction.

One evening, as the sun set over Bay City, Jack stood on the rooftop of the precinct, looking out over the city he had sworn to protect. Lisa joined him, her presence a comforting reminder of their partnership and shared mission.

"We did it, Jack," Lisa said, her voice filled with pride. "We brought down The Wolf."

Jack nodded, his eyes reflecting the weight of their journey. "Yeah, we did. But there's still work to be done."

Lisa smiled, her eyes filled with determination. "And we'll be here to do it. Together."

As the city lights began to twinkle in the twilight, Jack felt a renewed sense of purpose. The fight against crime and corruption was far from over, but he knew that with Lisa, Sarah, and their allies by his side, they could face whatever challenges lay ahead.

The future was uncertain, but their resolve was unbreakable. The battle for Bay City had been long and grueling, but they had emerged victorious. And they were ready to continue the fight, to protect their city and ensure that justice prevailed.

As the night settled over Bay City, Jack, Lisa, and Sarah stood ready, prepared to face whatever challenges lay ahead. The fight for Bay City had only just begun, and they were prepared to see it through to the end. The shadows of betrayal and corruption loomed large, but they knew that together, they could overcome any obstacle. They had faced the darkness and emerged stronger, their bond unbreakable and their mission clear.

The fight for Bay City was their mission, their purpose, and they would not rest until justice was served. The future was uncertain, but their resolve was unwavering. The battle for Bay City had only just begun, and they were prepared to see it through to the end.

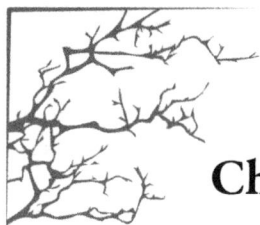

Chapter 15: A New Dawn

The first rays of dawn broke over Bay City, casting a golden glow over the skyline. The city was slowly waking up to a new day, one that carried the promise of hope and renewal. The battle against the crime syndicate had been long and grueling, but with the defeat of The Wolf and the dismantling of the syndicate, Bay City was finally beginning to heal.

Detective Jack Thompson stood on the rooftop of the precinct, looking out over the city he had sworn to protect. The events of the past few months played through his mind like a vivid montage – the relentless pursuit of justice, the harrowing battles, and the personal sacrifices that had marked their journey. The weight of those experiences sat heavily on his shoulders, but there was also a sense of accomplishment. They had done it. They had brought down the syndicate and restored a measure of peace to the city.

Jack was joined by his partner, Detective Lisa Ramirez, and Sarah Miller. The three of them had formed a bond forged in the fires of battle, their shared mission bringing them closer together. They stood side by side, each reflecting on the journey they had undertaken and the challenges that lay ahead.

"We did it," Lisa said, her voice tinged with both pride and exhaustion. "We brought down The Wolf and dismantled the syndicate. But it wasn't without cost."

Sarah nodded, her expression somber. "We lost good people along the way. Friends, colleagues. The price of justice is always high."

Jack remained silent for a moment, his gaze fixed on the horizon. "We knew what we were getting into. We knew the risks. But we also knew that we couldn't stand by and do nothing. The city needed us, and we answered the call."

The aftermath of the battle had been chaotic. The compound was a scene of devastation, with fires still smoldering and debris scattered everywhere. Emergency services had arrived quickly, tending to the wounded and securing the area. The news of The Wolf's death and the syndicate's downfall spread rapidly, bringing a sense of relief to a city that had been living in fear.

In the days that followed, Jack, Lisa, and Sarah worked tirelessly to dismantle the remnants of the syndicate's operations. They coordinated with the DEA, FBI, and other law enforcement agencies to track down and apprehend any remaining members. The task was daunting, but their resolve was unwavering.

One evening, as they sat in the precinct's conference room, reviewing case files and planning their next steps, Captain Reed entered the room. He had been a steadfast supporter throughout their mission, and his presence was a welcome sight.

"Jack, Lisa, Sarah," Reed said, his voice filled with pride. "I just wanted to take a moment to commend you on your work. What you've accomplished is nothing short of extraordinary. The city owes you a debt of gratitude."

Jack nodded, his expression serious. "Thank you, Captain. But we couldn't have done it without the support of the entire department and our allies."

Reed smiled. "Nevertheless, you three have been the driving force behind this operation. Your dedication and courage have made all the difference. Now, I know you're all eager to continue the fight, but I think it's important to take a moment to reflect on what you've achieved and to recognize the personal costs of this battle."

Lisa leaned back in her chair, her eyes reflecting the weight of those words. "It's been a long road, Captain. And it's not over yet. But we're ready for whatever comes next."

Sarah added, "The syndicate may be down, but crime doesn't just disappear. We'll need to stay vigilant and continue working to rebuild and protect this city."

Reed nodded. "I have no doubt that you'll rise to the challenge. But for now, take a moment to rest and reflect. You've earned it."

The following days brought a mix of emotions. The city was beginning to return to a semblance of normalcy, but the scars of the battle were still evident. Buildings needed to be repaired, businesses rebuilt, and communities healed. The police department worked around the clock to ensure that the transition was smooth and that any lingering threats were dealt with swiftly.

Jack took some time to visit the families of the officers who had fallen in the line of duty. It was a painful but necessary task, one that reminded him of the personal costs of their mission. He offered words of comfort and support, promising that their loved ones' sacrifices would never be forgotten.

Lisa and Sarah joined him on these visits, their presence a source of strength and solidarity. Together, they honored the memories of their fallen colleagues, vowing to continue the fight in their name.

One evening, as they sat in a quiet park, reflecting on the past and contemplating the future, Jack spoke up. "We've come a long way. We've faced down some of the worst that this city has to offer. But there's still so much work to be done."

Lisa nodded. "The fight against crime and corruption is never-ending. But we've shown that we can make a difference. We just need to keep pushing forward."

Sarah added, "And we need to remember why we do this. It's not just about bringing down the bad guys. It's about making this city a better place for everyone who lives here."

Jack smiled, a sense of resolve settling over him. "You're right. We've made a dent, but now it's time to build something better. A city where people can feel safe and where justice truly prevails."

The rebuilding process was slow but steady. The precinct became a hub of activity, with officers working tirelessly to restore order and provide support to the community. Jack, Lisa, and Sarah threw themselves into the effort, their dedication unwavering.

They also took time to address the deeper issues that had allowed the syndicate to thrive. They worked with community leaders, local businesses, and residents to develop programs aimed at preventing crime and providing opportunities for those at risk of falling into the criminal underworld.

One of their key initiatives was a youth outreach program, designed to provide mentorship and support to young people in vulnerable communities. Jack, Lisa, and Sarah took personal interest in the program, visiting schools, community centers, and organizing events to engage with the youth.

At one such event, held at a local community center, Jack stood before a group of teenagers, sharing his experiences and the importance of making positive choices.

"I know that life can be tough," Jack said, his voice filled with empathy. "I've seen firsthand how easy it is to get caught up in things that can lead you down the wrong path. But I want you to know that there are people who care about you and who want to help you succeed. We're here to support you, to guide you, and to show you that there are better options out there."

Lisa and Sarah joined him, sharing their own stories and offering words of encouragement. The response from the youth was overwhelmingly positive, and it became clear that the program was making a real difference.

As the weeks turned into months, the city continued to heal and rebuild. The efforts of Jack, Lisa, and Sarah were recognized not only by their colleagues but by the community as well. They were invited to speak at various events, their dedication and courage serving as an inspiration to many.

One afternoon, they were invited to City Hall, where the mayor presented them with commendations for their service. The ceremony was a solemn yet uplifting occasion, a testament to their hard work and sacrifice.

"As mayor of Bay City, it is my honor to recognize the outstanding efforts of Detectives Jack Thompson, Lisa Ramirez, and Sarah Miller," the mayor said, his voice filled with pride. "Their bravery and dedication have made our city a safer place. They have shown us what it means to be true public servants, and we are deeply grateful for their service."

Jack, Lisa, and Sarah accepted their commendations with humility, their hearts filled with a sense of purpose and fulfillment. They knew that their work was far from over, but they also knew that they had made a significant impact.

As they left City Hall, the three of them took a moment to reflect on their journey. They had faced incredible odds, endured unimaginable hardships, and emerged stronger and more united than ever.

"We've come a long way," Lisa said, her voice filled with pride. "But there's still so much more to do."

Jack nodded. "We can't rest on our laurels. We need to keep pushing forward, keep fighting for what's right."

Sarah smiled, her eyes filled with determination. "And we'll do it together. As a team."

In the months that followed, they continued their efforts to rebuild and protect Bay City. The precinct became a beacon of hope and justice, a place where officers worked tirelessly to serve and protect the community.

Jack, Lisa, and Sarah took on new cases, their resolve unshaken by the challenges they faced. They knew that the fight against crime and corruption was never-ending, but they also knew that they had the strength and determination to see it through.

As the city continued to heal, they saw firsthand the positive changes taking place. Communities were coming together, crime rates were dropping, and there was a renewed sense of hope and optimism.

One evening, as they sat in a quiet park, watching the sun set over the city, Jack spoke up. "We've made a difference. We've shown that it's possible to fight back and win. But we can't do it alone. We need the community, and we need each other."

Lisa nodded, her expression thoughtful. "And we need to remember why we do this. It's not just about bringing down the bad guys. It's about making this city a better place for everyone who lives here."

Sarah smiled, her eyes reflecting the strength of their bond. "And we'll do it together. As a team."

As the night settled over Bay City, the three of them sat in silence, reflecting on their journey and the challenges that lay ahead. The fight for justice was far from over, but they knew that with their unwavering resolve and the support of the community, they could face whatever came their way.

The future was uncertain, but their resolve was unbreakable. The battle for Bay City had been long and grueling, but they had emerged victorious. And they were ready to continue the fight, to protect their city and ensure that justice prevailed.

As the stars began to twinkle in the night sky, Jack, Lisa, and Sarah stood ready, prepared to face whatever challenges lay ahead. The fight for Bay City had only just begun, and they were prepared to see it through to the end. The shadows of betrayal and corruption loomed large, but they knew that together, they could overcome any obstacle.

The fight for Bay City was their mission, their purpose, and they would not rest until justice was served. As the night settled over the city, Jack, Lisa, and Sarah stood ready, prepared to face whatever challenges lay ahead. The future was uncertain, but their resolve was unwavering. The battle for Bay City had only just begun, and they were prepared to see it through to the end.

Don't miss out!

Visit the website below and you can sign up to receive emails whenever William James Brown publishes a new book. There's no charge and no obligation.

https://books2read.com/r/B-A-MCMXB-EQXIF

BOOKS 2 READ

Connecting independent readers to independent writers.

About the Author

William James Brown is a versatile author known for gripping thriller fiction, from espionage and psychological suspense to legal dramas and supernatural mysteries. His compelling narratives and unpredictable twists keep readers enthralled in the depths of human intrigue and suspenseful plots.

Milton Keynes UK
Ingram Content Group UK Ltd.
UKHW030142051224
452010UK00001B/207

9 798230 498711